BRIDGE BETWEEN
THE WORLDS

Maria Cowen

TABLE OF CONTENTS

CHAPTER 1

Hello! My name is David, and I am a SNYX. Only the most enlightened of you have ever heard of me before. I'll bet the first thing the rest of you are going to ask is, what is a SNYX? Well, it's an abbreviation for Super Natural Yav Expert, Yav standing for the highest grade of wisdom in the Universe. A Yav-10 rating is the best of the best. That's me, a Yav-10.

In order to rule, or shall I say, to govern a galaxy, it is necessary to achieve a rating of Yav-10. And it has taken me a long time to get where I am.

Right now, as I sit in the private suite which adjoins my office, I can permit myself a few moments of relaxation in which to let the memories flow freely. I am a very ancient being, more than just an old man, to use Terran vernacular. You'd never guess how old I am. I'm up for retirement now, and welcome the move to my peaceful estate in the country where I'll spend the rest of my days happily playing with my great, great, great grandchildren. But before I retire, I am obligated to give an account of my life in the form of a recorded autobiography, which "is accessible to future generations. It is the custom here. Perhaps no one will ever play these recordings after I am gone. But I am obliged to tell my story nonetheless.

(Excuse the interruption; I was distracted just then by an almost imperceptible sigh and wondered who was in the room, before I realized it must have come from me.)

To adjust my individual suspension system for maximum comfort, I shall take a moment to fine-tune the force bands on my chair until they reshape themselves to accommodate my girth, and then I'll stretch out my legs, leaning back to seemingly float on air. Glancing out of the window, I can't help but admire the tall, graceful spires, pointing at the sky. The gardens surrounding my Governor's mansion are planted with glorious Snevu, and the trees lining the T-shaped pool are in blossom, their creamy white flowers reflecting in the water.

The tranquility of my panorama contrasts starkly to the crazy traffic patterns overhead in the sky. Up there, commuters flock like thick swarms of birds against the late afternoon glow of twin suns. I can see big passenger rockets, cargo ferries, and many small private Voox units making their way home on autopilot. Only here in Rajpootu, capital of this galaxy, and busiest city in this part of the universe, could there be enough rush hour traffic to almost obliterate the sun. Closing my eyes, I let the images rush in, and as I looked longingly at the pristine countryside, I felt a rush of anticipation in the realization that I would soon be going home.

But first things first, and my autobiography

comes first. Adjusting the Memor-Tap headpiece I am wearing, I wonder how to begin. The Memor-Tap feels bulky, unfamiliar and uncomfortable. Oh well, the sooner I get on with it, the sooner I'll be done.

Relaxing in my chair, I let my mind drift back across the centuries, back to my early years on faraway Terra, the planet of my origin, as my memory unit noiselessly records every thought of long ago and far away...

Chapter 2

It was Saturday, early in the afternoon, and I looked out the window, wondering if it was going to rain. Rex, a big brown mongrel dog, must have been hunting in his sleep because his legs jerked and his ears and whiskers quivered. I was lying on my bed at the time, holding the remote control unit in my hand and playing a video game with languid expertise. Electronic bugs crawled down the screen of the display terminal and looked as if they were going to jump straight at my shoulder. I shot them down, one by one, until the last bug disintegrated, then I tossed the remote aside and lay back, closing my eyes.

If only I could be like other boys, I thought with bitterness and regret. If only I had the health and strength to play with other boys, or even to play like other boys!

While other boys hung around the drugstore after school, watching girls, riding skateboards, having fun, I sat at home in my room playing electronic games. How I envied all the boys who were normal. I was an oddity, a clumsy, painfully thin, twelve-year-old with an oversized head, flyaway ears, bottle-thick glasses and a thick covering of freckles. But, worse than that, my faulty immune system was the repository for every germ and infection going around. That's why Mom kept me indoors; it was the only way she could keep me healthy.

Needless to say, nobody liked me. They all called me a weirdo and a freak. The girls tried to pretend I wasn't there when I entered the classroom and the school bullies enjoyed every chance they got to jeer at me and push me around. I considered myself lucky that only twice, in twelve years, they'd broken my glasses, but I'd lost count of the times they'd punched me out or thrown stones at me to prove how much they hated the way I look. Different is not a good thing to be when you are a kid on Planet Terra.

If you're different, you're hated, you're punished for it, as if you could be goaded into becoming something more acceptable to other children. That's one of the unfortunate attitudes that cripples spiritual evolution on Terra to this day.

In those distant days of my youth, I had only one friend. He visited me two or three times a week. His name was Wang. He was a small, serious, Vietnamese boy who lived with his immigrant family in the apartments over on Peach Street. Wang's family was poor and, what was characteristic for that nation, very conservative. Wang greatly enjoyed playing my video games and experimenting with my computer.

The computer was a gift from my dad on my twelfth birthday, and it was the most important thing in my life. I simply loved discovering all its possibilities, and before long, had cracked all its codes and was quite familiar with its full potential by now. I would spend hours each day with my eyes glued to the screen and my fingers flying across the keyboard. Sometimes I would even get up in the middle of the night to play with my WOW, long after bedtime. I had to be very quiet about it, though, since Mom was very strict about such things. Anyway, my computer opened up a whole new world that enthralled me.

On that afternoon, I must have dozed off for a few minutes when I was jolted awake by my mother's voice. "David? Daveeee, dinner is ready!" I eased off the bed and ran downstairs. Rex had awakened from his own dappled slumber and was trying to beat me to the kitchen, almost knocking me down when he tried to run between my legs as I descended the stairs two steps at a time.

When there were no visitors, we usually ate at the big kitchen table. Dad was already sitting in his usual spot at the head of the table, while Mom juggled the pots and pans, dishing out portions of potatoes and stewed vegetables and meat onto dinner plates. My older sister, Doreen, came in through the outside kitchen door just then, slamming it shut behind her. I nearly jumped out of my skin, since I was a sensitive kid and loud noises bothered me. In fact, quite often a loud noise was enough to give me a searing headache.

Tonight I slouched into my chair and thought, Oh, no! Not corn chowder again! as my mother set a steaming bowl of the stuff in front of me. No use complaining though. I spooned up the chowder automatically, not caring to taste it. Corned beef, cabbage and boiled potatoes was the main course tonight. I managed to smuggle a few chunks of beef to Rex, under the table, where he waited, as usual, for whatever morsels I could sneak down to him. For dessert my mom served a jello. Rex didn't like jello, so I had to cope with it by myself.

Doreen was in a weird mood tonight. All through dinner, she made faces at me. At the ripe old age of fourteen, she considered herself to be an adult and therefore vastly superior to my humble self. I noticed that lately, when Mom wasn't around, she would put on mascara and lipstick, so as to impress her friends with how sophisticated and emancipated she had become. I can hardly wait for the day when Mom catches her in the act and gives her a good paddling on her emaciated rear.

Actually, Doreen was a pretty girl with light russet-brown hair that curled loosely to her shoulders, big blue eyes fringed with long dark lashes and a movie-star smile, when she was in good humor. The boys from our neighborhood would always stare and wolf-whistle when she walked by. How she got all the beauty and I got all the ugly was a phenomenon of never-ending perplexity to me. But then I guessed if the ugly genes had to be passed on to someone, it might as well be to the boy. I just couldn't imagine a girl having to go through life as ugly as me.

When dinner was over, my dad cleared his throat and tapped his water glass with his spoon. Doreen kicked me under the table. We both knew what was coming.

But this time we were wrong. It was Dad's custom, after dinner, to bore us all with his stories about what happened at the office, or about the news headlines covering the latest tragedy somewhere in the world. Usually, at such times, I would sit and try to think of some way to excuse myself and get back to my computer. But this time, Dad really surprised us. Clearing his throat again, he began to speak.

"Children, as you know, the school year will end in a couple of weeks. Well, your mother and I have discussed it and we agree it would be nice if you went to visit Grandma for a month or so. After all, she has been all alone in that big house since Grandpa died, and she must be very lonely. You two could lend her a hand around the place, as well as bring a little cheer into her life. What do you say? Would you like to spend a little time with Grandma?" He turned a hopeful face first towards Doreen and then to me.

Doreen made a face, as though she had just swallowed a maggot. Clearly, a visit to Grandma's house wasn't her idea of a fun summer. Neither was it mine. If I could take my computer with me, then there was a possibility. But if not, I decided I would refuse to go. Come to think of it, I would want to take Rex with me, too. In fact, the dog would probably be the only one to enjoy a summer in the country.

Dad was speaking again. ."Honestly, kids, I'm hoping you'll agree to go. How about a little break in the countryside?

"Your mom and I, well…, frankly, we need some rest from the old parenting routine, if you know what I mean."

I looked at him. It was true, he did need a rest; his face was tired and drawn. Obviously he had been pushing himself too hard. Perhaps it would be a good idea to give Mom and Dad a break. But did it have to be with Grandma?

Dad noticed the disappointment on our faces and urgently added, "Listen, kids, it'll only be for a few weeks. You'll enjoy it once you get there. Trust me!" He was half pleading now. Then there was a flicker in his eyes, as if he had a revelation. "Doreen, why don't you ask your girl-friend, Alice, to go with you? I'm sure Grandma wouldn't object, and your friend will be company for you. And you, David ... Hmmm. You can take Rex along, and your computer too... Why, you'll hardly know you've left home!"

"When would we have to go?" I was definitely doubtful about this idea, despite having permission to take my most precious possessions with me. "We'll drive you up to Grandma's place the weekend after school lets out. How about it?" He clearly expected some enthusiasm for his plan and, finding none, the light in his eyes flickered and died, to be replaced by disappointment.

"Aww, come on, kids! Why make it so difficult for us?" He crossed his arms over his chest and looked defeated and even more tired than before. Suddenly I felt sorry for my attitude. How could I be so selfish when my dad was asking for such a small favor?

"Gee, Dad, I haven't seen Gran since I was nine years old. And she is getting pretty old. Maybe it'll be our last chance to spend some time with her. I guess it won't be so bad, if I can take Rex and my computer." The light flickered back on behind Dad's eyes.

"Yes," I said firmly. "The more I think about it, the more I like the idea. And as far as I'm concerned, Doreen and her weird friend can go to China this summer. Who needs 'em? I'll visit Gran by myself!"

Doreen looked daggers at me. She must have thought I'd suddenly gone stark, raving mad, agreeing to go to visit Grandma so spontaneously. And Dad, seeing that he had won me over, turned his persuasive powers upon his unwilling daughter.

"Dori, your brother doesn't mean that. Say you'll go, too! with or without your girlfriend. Okay? For me? Say you'll go, too."

"What? I thought you said I could invite Alice?" She was hooked by his take-away. "If I can't invite Alice, I won't go!"

"Alice? Oh, sure. Invite her along. But if she can't go, I hope you'll plan on accompanying your brother anyway."

Doreen lowered her head in resignation, a gesture which Dad took for agreement.

"Good! It's all settled, then. Plan to leave on the first Saturday after school lets out." He spread his daily paper on the table before him, thus dismissing us and ending the discussion.

I dashed up to my room, hotly pursued by Rex, who dived for the bed a heartbeat behind me, where we tumbled around for a while.

That night, as I drifted off to sleep, it occurred to me that the summer program wasn't going to be such a bad one, after all. Gran's house was surrounded by rolling meadows and green pastures. Grandpa used to breed horses there, and I hoped there were a few left on the place to ride. I loved animals, felt a special kinship with them. Suddenly I found myself looking forward to summer vacation with unprecedented eagerness.

CHAPTER 3

It was a hot, sunny day and our old Ford jumped, squeaked and protested as Dad guided it down the pot-holey road. Actually, it wasn't so much a road as a trail of twin ruts, decorated with tree roots and rabbit holes, which crossed the fields to Grandma's place. Despite the new shocks Dad had just installed on the Ford, it was a rough ride.

"We're almost there," Dad spoke to reassure Mom, who was holding tight to the door handle in order to keep herself from bouncing all over the front seat. I saw that she was looking out at the rolling green hills with a nostalgic smile on her face. This was her childhood home, these were her fields and grassy meadows through which trickled cool streams, and this pastoral scene would be forever etched on her memory.

Not bad, I thought, it's very scenic out here. I leaned my face against the rear side window, causing my glasses to clatter against the pane.

Next to me sat Doreen and her friend, Alice, oblivious to the sweeping panorama as they twittered and giggled at one another over their magazines. Whoops! The car shook violently as two tires dropped into a rut and we all fell to one side. I was glad that my computer was secured in the trunk wrapped in several layers of blanket, and I silently prayed it would arrive at our destination with all parts intact.

"Sssssshhhh," Doreen hissed as the car lurched again and she massaged one elbow and threw me the look of a wounded wildcat.

"Grandma's house is in the valley just behind this next hill," Mother informed us happily, as though we were visiting this place for the very first time.

"We should arrive just in time for dinner," added Dad, always the practical thinker.

Suddenly the engine coughed and died.

"What the hell" Dad restrained himself from swearing in the presence of minors and got out of the car. Walking around to the front, he opened the hood. Clouds of white vapour enveloped him as the old radiator overheated and blew off steam.

Dad waved for us all to get out. "Might as well stretch our legs while we wait for the engine to cool off enough for me to top up this radiator with fresh water," he said.

The meadows smelled fragrantly of fresh grass, herbs and sweet earth. Insects were buzzing happily around the wildflowers as though they hadn't a care in the world. The minute I opened the car door the lenses of my glasses hazed over with vapor and I realized that it was very hot out here compared to the air conditioned car interior.

After removing my glasses to polish them on

the hem of my T-shirt, I went to check on my computer in the trunk. It looked very comfortable, all swathed in blankets like that.

I just hoped nothing had jarred loose during the ride.

Mom distributed drinks from the portable cooler and I took my paper cup of lemonade off some distance to lay down on the grass and watch the insects. There were hundreds of different bugs, beetles, ants, flying insects and crawling things all busily pursuing their daily routine. I could easily have studied them for hours on end, just trying to figure out what they were up to. When a black and yellow bumblebee buzzed around my ear, I didn't flinch; I wasn't afraid of it. Something told me the little guy wasn't going to sting if I asked him not to. Then I stretched out one hand and a ladybug flew onto it, lighting on my palm. I watched her as she walked up and down my arm for a while, then she stopped to daintily wash her face.

"David? Where are you? Daveee!" The voice of my mother broke the spell. "Daveee, it's time to go!"

"Over here, Mom. Keep your shirt on, I'm coming!" I returned reluctantly to the car. Oh well, I'd have all the time in the world to study the flora and fauna of these meadows once things settled down.

"Davy, I know you're going to be happy here. This place was just made for a boy to explore. Why don't you plan to stay all summer?" Gran brushed back a tendril of white hair, which had escaped from her bun, as she spoke. She crinkled her face at me in a warm smile and looked at me with those eyes, which were such a surprising blue. I had never seen such clear, brilliant light blue except in the sky at certain times of day. I slid a look over at Doreen and saw panic clearly written on her face. She was afraid she'd be coaxed into spending the entire summer, too.

"Oh, Gran. We'd like to stay the whole summer, but we absolutely must get back to other commitments after a week or two," she breathed in her most sophisticated voice. "You see, we definitely must be back in the city by the Fourth of July." Doreen cast a quick glance in the direction of her friend, Alice, and a look of understanding passed between them.

"And what calls you back to the city so soon, my dear?" Gran wasn't one to take no for an answer. She fixed my sister with a calm but penetrating look.

"Well, we .... Uh, we ... "stammered Doreen, "we want to do some things of importance.." She faltered. She clearly had not prepared herself for this interrogation and her retort was weak and hazy.

"What sorts of things, dear?" asked Gran, sweetly but insistently.

"Now, what do you think a couple of teenaged girls want to do back in the city, Grandma?" Dad finished the lentil soup and pushed his plate away. "Fool around with boys, of course! These girls are a bit boy crazy, if you ask me."

"Well, there's no need to rush into any decisions." Mom tried to smooth things over before Doreen exploded in tears and ran from the table, as was her custom every time Dad even looked at her sideways. "Maybe you girls will come to like it here," she added hopefully. "After all, I grew up here and it's not such a bad place, you know." She looked at her scornful daughter with reproach. "At any rate, that's enough· said for now. You've just arrived and it's hardly fitting to be talking about going back home before you've even unpacked."

"Hmmm." Both girls sighed in doubtful resignation to the situation at hand.

We were all seated around the big old oak table in Granny's dining room. The table was laden with food in celebration of our arrival. In the center was a compote of shiny red apples, frosty blue grapes and juicy pears. Next to the compote was a breadboard holding a loaf of hot, fresh country bread and a pot of butter. Next to that was Gran's homemade elderberry wine in a crystal decanter, and in the place of honor sat a huge platter bearing a prime rib roast which had just been carried in from the kitchen by Gran's housekeeper, Anna Boggs.

Anna Boggs was a chunky peasant woman in her late forties. She was as strong as an ox, wore straw-blond braids and had red cheeks to match the bows on her hair. Anna practically ran Gran's house and the farm singlehandedly, and Mom always said she didn't know how Gran could manage to live out here in the country in her declining years if she ever lost Anna's services.

Right now Anna was slicing up the prime rib and placing each slice on a plate so it could be passed down the table. After that, she would return to the kitchen and reappear bearing bowls of broccoli in cheese sauce, gravy, mashed potatoes, and French fries to choose from. I looked at the feast before me and wondered if my stomach was big enough to put it all away.

We all ate in silence for a time. After Anna took away my dinner plate, I had a chance to look around the room while everyone else went back for seconds. There was a huge, old-fashioned fireplace on the east wall, which was never used during the summer. Grandpa's trophy display of mounted deer antlers took up the whole of the north wall, and the west side of the room was lined with French windows which opened onto a spectacular view and the rays of the setting sun which bathed the room in gold and crimson light. Then, I noticed something new. Moving into my range of view came dark clouds on the horizon, rolling in from an easterly direction, moving fast as if pushed along by a mighty wind. storm clouds! I loved storms, although I couldn't explain why.

As though she could read my thoughts, Gran said, "Last year during one of our summer electrical storms, the lightning struck a tree right behind this house. We were lucky that it didn't burn, because the buildings could have caught fire. Our storms can get pretty wild and wooly at times, children, but if you stay indoors you'll be okay."

Dad had been engrossed in mopping up the last of the gravy from his plate. Now he straightened up and dabbed at the corners of his mouth with a napkin, as he prepared to join the conversation.

"I remember one bad storm, when I was just a kid up north, when my family lived in.... " he began.

Ufff, I thought. He's winding UP to tell another of his boring stories. Somebody kicked me under the table just then, and Rex licked my hand. I patted Rex and pushed his nose down to keep him quiet. There was no way I could smuggle any meat to him right under Gran's nose. I would be seen, and I would catch it. Anyway, Anna would feed my hound a handsome meal of leftovers in the kitchen after dinner.

Then I felt another kick, a strong one that left my right shin smarting. Doreen was signaling to me to make my excuses and leave the room, so she could do the same. She was no dummy; she knew that if I got permission to leave, they wouldn't be likely to force her to remain behind.

When Dad's story trailed off temporarily, while he watched Anna pour elderberry wine into his goblet, I seized the moment and spoke out.

"Dad? I'm too full for desert right now, so may I please be excused to go and visit the horses before it gets dark?

Dad nodded and waved me out of the room, so I jumped to my feet and mumbled, "Excuse me, Dad. Thanks for the good meal, Gran," and "Be back before dark, Mom." Then I ran for the French doors with Rex at my heels. Dad was already into his story when I looked back to see Doreen and Alice, trapped into listening before they could break away, with expressions of desperation and hatred focused on me. And I knew I'd hear about it from Doreen later. No doubt she'd berate me for not leaping to my feet the first time she kicked me. Too bad.

Rounding the house, I headed out back where

the stables were. A peculiar odor was in the air and it got stronger as I got closer to the barn. The barn doors were slightly ajar, and as I entered, the odor became heavy in the air. I recognized it now; it was the odor of hay and horses, all mingled together.

Inside, there was a long row of stalls where many horses had once been kept, but now only half were occupied. Obviously, the horse breeding business wasn't good. I just remembered Mom telling Dad that it was a shame Gran hadn't the strength or interest to keep the business up now that Granddad was gone. I strolled along the corridor outside the stalls until suddenly I felt attracted to one horse in particular. She was gazing at me with large, limpid brown eyes, and her dappled grey coat shone in the dim light of the barn as she tossed her mane and whinnied softly at me.

Moving closer, I stretched out one hand in the direction of her nostrils. She sniffed it, her nostrils flaring gently, and tossed her head. I reached around to caress her beautiful, long mane and when she gave a little groan of approval, I knew that we were friends. I could hear the other horses moving restlessly in their stalls, curious about what was happening.

I should have remembered to bring a handful of sugar cubes, I thought in reproach, and decided to return to the kitchen and get some right then. So, returning to the house, I entered through the kitchen door. Big Anna was washing dishes.

She turned to look at me as though I had no business intruding upon her space.

"Hi, there." I tried the friendly approach. She turned to face me and placed her hands on her wide hips, waiting, menacingly, for how I was going to explain this invasion of her territory.

"Uh," I faltered, not intimidated into meekness. "Uh, I just came in to see if I could find some sugar cubes for the horses." Anna relaxed and her face dimpled into a big smile.

"Horses! Why sure, sonny, take the whole bowl if you want. Those horses haven't had their sweet tooth pampered in a long while."

Evidently she wasn't as formidable as she looked. I grabbed a handful of sugar cubes, stuffed them in my pocket and thanked her as I backed out the kitchen door. Then I returned to the stables.

Night had fallen when I emerged from the barn. I remembered that I had promised to return before dark, and hoped that Dad was still telling his story, and no one would notice it had gotten dark. Then a twinkle caught my eye, and I looked up to see a big clear patch of sky studded with the most brilliant assortment of stars I had ever seen in my life.

Wow! You sure can't see stars like this in the city, I thought. Teacher once mentioned that air pollution prevents it. But there they are, in all their glory, shining just for me! I wished I'd remembered to bring my telescope. There was Orion, and the Pleiades ... I clearly recognized all the familiar stars and clusters. Crickets sang their evening song to me from the grass, and it was an enchanted moment that would remain in my memory for many years to come.

This was my first glimpse of the infinite, deeply touching and very special.

Entering Gran's house through the kitchen, I was struck by the thought that I had not had my dessert, and when Anna came bustling back through the swinging door, she found me sitting at the table,. ready to ask for a piece of lemon meringue pie. Rex had long since departed my company and stuffed his furry belly with a fine meal of leftovers before collapsing in a corner of the kitchen to snooze. Luckily, when Mom came through the kitchen door to ask Anna for a headache tablet and saw me sitting at the table, eating pie and drinking milk, she never thought to ask what time I'd come back from the barn. I heaved a sigh of relief, thinking, "Somebody up there must like me."

After watching some television in the big, comfortable living room, Gran assigned us to our sleeping quarters and Anna led us, single-file, up the big curving staircase, each carrying his own duffle bag. I liked my room at once; it had a big window facing east and a large table just under it which was perfect for my computer. Doreen and Alice were assigned a twin-bedded room at the far end of the corridor, while my parents, who were here for the weekend, were going to sleep on the divan in the den, downstairs.

There was no use asking Dad to help me lug the computer up to my room until morning, so I unpacked my duffle and stowed my clothing. Then I got ready for bed and opened the window to let in some fresh air. Not sleepy yet, I sat on the wide parapet, looking at the sky. Then I spotted a shooting star, and another! I closed my eyes and quickly made a wish. I wished that someday I could go to the stars and learn about the people who lived on them in my exploration of the heavens. I knew it was an improbable wish, but who ever said wishes had to make sense? It never occurred to me that this wish would come true a lot sooner than I could imagine in my wildest dreams.

On Sunday, Mom and Dad drove back to the city right after lunch, leaving us three adolescents under the supervision of Gran and Anna. In the dappled late afternoon sunlight of succeeding days, I explored the neighboring hills astride Phaedra, my noble steed, and Doreen and Alice sunbathed beside the stream while they chatted and read aloud from romance magazines and pretended they were adults.

On the first morning following our arrival, the girls had met Tommy, the stable boy, who took his breakfast every day in the kitchen. He was a tall, well-built high school grad and it was obvious they developed an immediate crush on him, for they trailed him around, ogling and twittering like idiots, until Anna scolded that they were not letting the poor boy get his chores done. Considering that Tommy was eighteen, I could imagine he had better things to do than fool around with a couple of addlepated pubescent girls.

As the days flew by in sunny harmony, to my great surprise, I began to feel much healthier in the country than I ever had back home. In the city, I spent most of my time nursing sniffles and allergies, when I wasn't hiding out from the other kids and keeping to my room to avoid their scorn and derision. But here at Gran's, I felt strong, healthy and free. Nobody looked at me like they thought I was weird. For once, I could really relax.

Before supper on my second afternoon at the

ranch, I asked Gran if I could take Phaedra, her dappled mare, for a walk. Gran wasn't confident of my ability to handle a horse, so she called Tommy and asked him to be my instructor and teach me all about horses and how to ride. In spite of my spindly, puny physique, I was dying to learn horsemanship, and Tom was just the amiable sort to teach me. But how could Gran have guessed? I concluded that my grandmother was a magical person who could read my mind whenever she chose.

Every day after that, Tommy, Phaedra and I spent the mornings together, training and practicing riding techniques. This was followed by a good grooming for the mare. Phaedra was patient and cooperative as I gradually learned to stay balanced on her back. And after one week, I was galloping joyfully through the pastures on her back. This newly cultivated skill had me bursting with pride. It was the very first thing of a physical nature that I had ever accomplished, and I could feel" the muscles in my arms and legs expanding and rippling with newfound strength.

My appetite developed along with my horsemanship, and Anna began to take special pride in the way I was plumping out, attributing it to her cooking. Best of all, I was gaining a good suntan, except ·for my nose which was always blistered, despite the zinc ointment Gran slathered on. The weeks passed in a chain of endlessly sunny days that I hoped would last forever. Unfortunately, this wasn't going to be the case.

CHAPTER 4

Regarding the ill-fated day of my disappearance, I can recall every detail with unusual crispness and clarity. I awoke that morning to a rainy drizzle topped off by an overcast that looked like it had settled in for the rest of the summer. At breakfast, Gran mentioned that it was going to be necessary to light the fireplace tonight to take the chill off the evening, even though it had not been lit at this season for twenty years. Then she called for Tommy and ordered him to fill up the wood bin beside the hearth and set the kindling wood and paper wicks ready for the strike of a match.

After breakfast, I played with my computer for most of the morning and then, in spite of the weather, I decided to saddle Phaedra and go for a ride. We both needed some fresh air. Down the big old staircase I went, taking it two steps at a time. This was quite an accomplishment for me in contrast to my stumbling awkwardness back at home. Even under my frail frame, the weathered treads groaned and creaked as I jumped lightly along. On my way through the kitchen, I grabbed a handful of sugar cubes, which I buttoned into my shirt pocket under my windbreaker to keep them from melting in the rain, and on second thought, doubled back for another handful of peanut butter cookies for myself.

Anna surprised me when she entered and caught me pulling my hand from the cookie jar. She opened her mouth to say something, but I caught her look of reproach and fled out the back door before she could say one word.

If there was a sun out there somewhere, it must have been shining on the uppermost layers of cloud, because it was very shadowy on the fields. Instead of ten o'clock in the morning, it seemed more like ten o'clock in the evening on a midsummer's day, when almost all the light has left the sky.

As I crossed the yard to the barn, the grass squished soggily under my sneakered feet, and on the gravel path I had to dodge little puddles of rain, which threatened to form a narrow creek with a gravel bottom. From the looks of things, it must have been raining all night.

In the barn, Phaedra greeted me enthusiastically and tossed her head like a sassy young filly, impatient for me to release her from her stall. I stroked her nose and treated her to some sugar cubes, and she danced around and nuzzled me, snorting her thanks.

"Hi, Dave. Are you here to take her out for a little canter?" Tommy appeared with a forkful of hay. At my nod, he added, "Just keep your britches on and I'll saddle her up for you 'in a jiffy."

"No hurry," I replied. "I can wait." And I

walked down the line of stalls, greeting the other horses in order to kill some time.

When Tommy had Phaedra all saddled up, he whistled me over and offered me a leg-up. I was' glad he was there; without him I would have had to balance on the railing while I saddled her because I was much too short in stature to handle it from the ground; not to mention the fact that I had never considered how I would mount her without a ladder or some help like that. Thanking Tommy, I waved goodbye and rode out into the gloom, Phaedra's hooves kicking up the water along the pathway as we went. Today my 'steed was really eager to go; she was straining against the reins and I had some trouble holding her to a brisk trot.

Suddenly, Rex came tearing around the side of the house, barking wildly as if to chide us for leaving without him. He was a big dog, and had no trouble catching up. Together, we cantered across the meadow, through the stream and up the other bank. Gran's pasture land runs the length and breadth of gentle sloping foothills which were lightly forested in the gullies. Today it was my goal to reach the lake on the other side of the farthest forest, and explore its rim. In less than half an hour we were nearly there. I could see the lake through the trees, shaped like a horseshoe or maybe a crescent moon, and leaned forward, pressing my cheek to Phaedra's silky neck, letting her run the rest of the way.

Her long, feathery mane streamed in the wind and soon my face was tickled with the feel of corn tassels, while my nose was filled with the smell of her sweat.

Reaching the lake, I reined Phaedra in and brought her to a halt. Letting her reins drop, I watched as she lowered her graceful head and drank long and deeply from the rippling, opaque water. After a while of letting Phaedra wander aimlessly, munching on grasses that grew by the water's edge, I took up the reins again and turned her toward a new forest that was now visible in the distance to the east. Some inexplicable urge was irresistibly drawing me further and further from my grandma's home, and I felt powerless to resist.

We're going to have an electrical storm again, soon, I thought, as I looked up at the billowing clouds that were growing black with condensation. Then I nudged Phaedra into a canter and we set out across the fields to the forest beyond. We must have cantered for an hour before we reached the first line of tall pines and cedars. I climbed out of the saddle and slid to the ground, an act I immediately regretted as I found myself wondering how I'd ever be able to remount.

Rex jumped on me and licked my face joyously at being in contact with me again after all this time. After calming down fifty pounds of jumping fur and what seemed like several feet of pink tongue, I grasped Phaedra's halter and led her into the forest. The ground was carpeted by a spongy layer of soft needles and a thick canopy of branches nearly obliterated the sky, with the exception of a gap here and there through which I could see a menacing cover of foreboding grey. Around me, all was silent in the mysterious forest twilight.

Time seemed to stand still as we walked together, deeper into the woods. The trees grew together more tightly now and sometimes there was barely enough space between their trunks for Phaedra to walk through. It never occurred to me how careless and foolish I was to be venturing deeper into this forest. Suddenly I observed thick, curling vines descending from high branches as if the forest itself wanted to capture me and draw me into the unknown. I felt chilled and suddenly defensive. I decided it was time to turn back. But which way should I go? Whichever way I walked, it seemed as though I had never passed that way before.

Am I lost? The thought horrified me. Noooo! Now, let's see ... I'm quite sure we came from over ... from over ... there! I led Phaedra and Rex in a new direction, only to find myself half an hour later in an even less familiar part of the forest.

No, I will not cry! Only babies cry. I got a firm hold on my quavering resolve. surely I can find my way out of here, somehow!

After a couple of hours of pointless circling, I gave up. Despite the fact that it was only five o'clock, it was getting dark now and I was frankly terrified. I knew if I didn't return home by suppertime, Gran would become alarmed and send Tommy to search for me. But how could he possibly manage to find me so far from home, and in the dark?

I wondered what sorts of creatures lived in this forest. wild pigs? Rabbits? What else? Wolves? Bears? Brrr! No, I won't think about it, I resolved, as we wandered into a large clearing. Looping Phaedra's reins around a tree, I decided to explore the clearing in the dying light. The area appeared to be as big as a stadium.

Then darkness closed in. No moon or stars were visible through the heavy cloud cover. The sky looked fathomless and black. Visibility was zero, and only the cold nose of my dog nuzzling into my hand reassured me that I was not alone. Good old Rex. If it hadn't been for him, I might have broken down and sobbed in sheer hysteria. Instead, I sat down on the ground and tried to feel around with my hands for a comfortable patch of grass on which to lie. Then, curling myself around Rex for warmth, I closed my eyes and waited for morning.

CHAPTER 5

I must have been exhausted from my ordeal. Must have instantly fallen asleep. How long I slept is anyone's guess. I had no idea what time it was when I fell asleep since the watch I was wearing didn't have a luminous dial. Gradually, a strange humming sound penetrated the veil of my dreams and its relentless urgency brought me fully awake. When I opened my eyes, I thought, at first, that it was morning, since the clearing was bathed in a cool light. I sat up and focused my eyes on my watch. The digital read-out said 3:55 a.m. Then I saw what I took to be a mirage. I thought, "This can't be real!" Pinching myself painfully to make sure I was awake, I rubbed my eyes and looked again.

An enormous blue phosphorescent disk floated effortlessly above me over the clearing, some twenty feet above the ground. Wow! Could it be? A real flying saucer! Holy smoke! I wasn't afraid any more. Somehow I sensed that whoever piloted the UFO had no intention of hurting me. How I knew this, I couldn't say, but I felt secure in this knowledge just the same.

I scrambled to my feet. The ship cast a silvery-blue, elusive light over the forest and the clearing, turning it all into a fantasy land. Rex flattened himself flat on the ground and whined softly with fear. I leaned over and scratched him behind the ear to reassure him that everything was just fine. The humming noise grew stronger and the disk seemed to be descending lower and lower.

"Gosh, it's going to land!" I thought, as my heart quickened its pace. Squatting down on my haunches, I hugged Rex around the neck and watched with unbelieving eyes.

The disk slowly descended to the ground and set down right in the middle of the clearing. I could hardly believe what was happening right in front of me. I stood there, transfixed and hardly daring to breathe. Not knowing what to do, I did nothing. I simply waited. Whoever or whatever was inside that disk was waiting, too. Several minutes passed without incident.

Then the oval hatch opened, exposing a very brightly lighted interior. Still, I waited. Nobody emerged. Are they waiting for me to go aboard? I wondered. Very slowly, I approached the ship with Rex slinking along one step behind me. I had to shield my eyes against the brightness of the lights glowing from the disk, for the closer I came, the brighter it was. The hatch was only a few yards away now, and it was six or seven feet above the ground. Well, that settles it. There's no stairs or ramp, so I can't very well get inside!

Nevertheless, I inched closer and closer to the ship. The humming noise was very irritating at this range, and I guessed this was due to its frequency rather than having to do with volume. I covered my ears with my hands to diminish the sound, and narrowed my eyes to keep the light from blinding me while I shuffled still nearer to the ship.

Suddenly, an invisible force lifted me from the ground and effortlessly floated me upward into the hatch. I began to cry in alarm. After all, I was only twelve years old.

Then I was deposited gently on the hatchway floor to stand there uncertainly, trying to catch my breath, which was hiccupping from the sobs.

When I calmed down, I noticed there was nothing but brightness inside. I wished I had my dark sunglasses with me; the ones I usually took along on rides when Phaedra and I galloped straight into the sun. But yesterday had been gloomy, and the glasses were still in my room at Gran's. I recalled all this as if it had happened a minute ago; I remember that distinctly.

Abruptly, the ship's lights dimmed and began pulsating with a strange, hypnotic regularity as the hatchway hummed and clicked closed. The new sound was monotonous, but appealing to my ears, and I felt that I was sinking into some kind of a dreamy trance, like when the doctor put me to sleep to take my adenoids out, despite my efforts to stay awake. The last thing I remember was the wetness of Rex's tongue licking my hand. Then I melted into the light.

CHAPTER 6

I awoke to find myself stretched prone on a hard surface with my ears open and my eyes shut, I immediately sensed that I was not in my room at Gran's house. And then I remembered getting lost in the forest and being awakened by the UFO. My head throbbed, but other than that, my body felt okay. I opened my eyes, tried to focus, saw nothing. Was I blind? Had the brilliant lights injured my eyes? I felt panic and tried to raise my hands to my eyes but could not move them. Tugging, I sensed that they were bound to the sides of the furniture upon which I lay.

"He has awakened." The voice spoke in a foreign dialect, which I somehow understood, and came from somewhere to my right. It was a gentle, melodious voice, but I couldn't tell if it belonged to a male or a female.

"What incredible luck! It has been a very long time since we've come across a specimen like this one. He is a natural SNYX. With the abilities and sensitivities we are registering, it is exciting to think how well he could benefit from training. Why, in short order, he could easily replace Yav-5 and maybe even Yav-6," rejoined someone to my left.

"But Taaz," urged the voice to my right, "we must not forget the law of restricted planets; pick up specimen, examine specimen, erase memory, return specimen to location of discovery, and leave no trace of ever having visited the planet."

"Yes, yes, I know," responded the voice to my left. "But how can we allow such a rare talent to be wasted?"

I tried to speak to these beings but my throat muscles would not move. Was I drugged? Was I hallucinating? What was preventing me from moving or seeing or even talking?

"I will transmit a special petition to HQ requesting permission to bring this one in for further observation. After all, if our superiors do not agree with my proposed induction, we can always erase memory and return the subject to this place."

"Holy cow! What is going on here, anyway? Am I dreaming, or what?" I wondered why my head wouldn't quit aching, and since I had no other choice, I waited to learn what would happen next.

"All right," said a voice on my right. "I'll consider it, Taaz. Now let's unhook the subject from the sensor panel and let him circulate with the others for the time being."

Before I could wonder about the so-called sensor panel and how I was supposedly hooked up to it, I felt myself sinking into a fuzzy sort of greyness which enveloped my brain and put me to sleep again.

When I awoke again, I was reclining on a soft

contour divan in a room containing other humans who had been brought on board for examination. There were three other boys, like me, between the ages of five to fourteen, and a collection of rural men and women. When I spoke to one of the boys and wondered aloud whether my dog, Rex, had been beamed aboard with me, I received only a blank look. However, some hidden microphone must have monitored my question, because instantly a video screen lit up beside me which displayed a cabin lined with glass-like cages of all sizes, containing dogs, cats, sheep, and Rex! I saw that my dog looked comfortable and relaxed, so I involuntarily thanked the unseen cameraman out loud and the picture clicked off.

I wondered to myself whether the animals were the subjects' of experimentation and the realization came to me that all the animals would be returned to their home turf and would experience no harmful after-effects from their quarantine and observation. How did I know this? This feeling of reassurance was welcome, though baffling.

Time went by and, although I could relax and remote-tune an infinite number of channels from my planet on my contour lounge-mounted TV, and watch the others or talk to them at will, I did not meet a single alien being. Needless to say, this was a major disappointment. Whenever instruction was given, it was given telepathically to me, and through radio headsets worn by all the others. I was asked questions to which I replied out loud at first. Then I realized they could read my thoughts, and I saved my breath. This was kind of scary.

It occurred to me that if I thought one thing and said another, they would read my mind and know both sides of the reply. It put an end to mental privacy, and somehow this offended me more than the act of being held captive. On the other hand, this telepathic gift of theirs could be very useful. I discovered that all I had to do was want for food or drink, or whatever creature comfort crossed my mind, and it was supplied. Obviously, we were being monitored on a continuous basis.

When I asked about Phaedra, who I'd left helplessly tied to a tree, I was told not to worry because a male human had arrived on horseback at the clearing the following morning and taken Phaedra away. That must have been Tom. This news relaxed me somewhat. I don't know why, but I believed them implicitly.

I had no idea how long I was there, as there was no night or day in this constant ambience. I noticed that our little group was dwindling in number and asked about it in my thoughts. The reply came, that they were being returned to their places of origin, one by one, as their examinations came to a close. They would remember nothing except maybe in their dreams.

When I was the only one left in the cabin, the announcement came that I was to stay and accompany them, if I wished to do so. They said they had waited for special permission to remove me from this planet, if I would agree to go. Permission from whom? I wondered. They said on their world I would be admired for my talents and not made to suffer the prejudice of unevolved beings, as I had in my native environment. How could they know? Assuming it would be a brief trip to visit an advanced culture, I asked if Rex could go with me. The answer was no. They were obliged to return Rex to the ground, they said. I wailed and argued with my unseen hosts, to no avail. They could not understand what I meant when I said he had to be with me because he was my dog. Gently, firmly, they insisted they did not have permission to remove the canine unit from its habitat and that he had to go back. They told me not to worry, because Rex would be just fine without me.

Then, at my insistence, they let me say goodbye. A door slid soundlessly open and Rex entered my cabin. I cried until my eyes were all puffy and Rex's ruff was soaked with tears. Then I had to let him go. The door slid open again and, bidden by an unheard command, Rex turned away from me and trotted out. Alone now, in the big cabin, I wondered what to do. I missed Gran and Rex and Anna and Tom. I even missed my sister, in spite of myself. And I wondered if and when I would ever see Mom and Dad again, and this made me feel very sad. In fact, a couple of times I came very close to demanding that they put me back, too. But the excitement of visiting an alien planet kept me half-interested in what lay ahead.

The aliens kept out of sight, but they really tried to make me feel good. They said I'd be enrolled at the Academy on Teenpon, where I was destined to study many subjects of importance to my future. When I replied that I was too young to attend an academy, and had not yet graduated from high school, they said it didn't matter at all. They said the only thing that mattered was the level of intelligence, whether one was human, saurian, or xooth. I wondered what "saurian" and "xooth" could mean, but no answer came.

I was informed that the ship would arrive on Teenpon in one week by my time calculation, and that in the meantime, I would learn about and prepare to meet other forms of life which were different from life forms as I knew them. During this time, they also advised that I would undergo a simple and very minor surgical procedure on the brain in which they would add a few neurons that would enable me to communicate freely with other life forms in the galaxy, telepathically.

They assured me I would soon be able to communicate with pure energy forms as well.

Wow! I could hardly wait!

The operation was entirely painless and efficiently performed, although I could only guess at the technique used according to their level of technical sophistication at that time. When it was done, I was able to hop off the table and function as usual, with no after-effects. The difference was, that although I communicated with these beings telepathically, now I had an active sense of participation. I could read their thoughts whenever I wanted to, and not just when they were replying to my unspoken question or planting a thought in my mind. Perhaps the most thrilling part of opening my eyes after the operation was that I could now see my hosts as well. I recall the sight was a shock, at first, but not for long.

When I recalled my comic book images of alien people, I had to chuckle at the notion that they would be very small-bodied with large, slanted eyes, or ten feet tall with the wings of angels. The crew on board this ship was a cross-section of different races from the far corners of the universe. It would be really a task to try to describe them all. But to mention just a few, there were Ninoohs from the planet zeta: good-natured, chunky, bearlike beings with round, soft, intelligent brown eyes and long, shiny fur. Then there were Sylvans from planet Thoon: quarrelsome, small, ugly beings with wrinkled hairless upper bodies and smooth hides from the waist down, all covered with a fine growth of long, rusty hair to their hoofed feet. And last, but not least, there were the Wyrinx from Talaira: graceful creatures whose wings would spread to reflect all the dazzling, luminous colors of the rainbow. I soon made friends with them all, and there was a certain sadness felt by the crew when we landed on Teenpon and had to part.

CHAPTER 7

The Academy was a much larger complex than I expected. It lay in the northern hemisphere of the planet Teenpon, bordering a beautiful emerald ocean. The main administrative buildings were a pyramid shape constructed of grey stone flecked with particles of a shiny mineral trapped within. The effect was truly charming when the sun's rays bounced off the buildings and caused them to shine with millions of refracted points of brilliance.

The maze of classrooms, laboratories, lecture halls and other facilities, whose function and purpose I couldn't begin to guess, were interconnected with graceful arches and walkways adorned with plants and blossoming shrubs. The panorama of the campus was enriched by wide stretches of well-watered grass, green squares with trees and benches, and several dancing fountains. The water sparkled and shimmered in the sun. "Tox" was the name given to the sun of Teenpon; it contained ten times the mass of the yellow sun shining back on Terra, therefore when the sun was at its zenith, it was necessary to remain indoors or inside a vehicle shielded against the burning rays.

All facilities at the Academy were climate controlled for maximum comfort. The proctor, an old, withered being of a race I couldn't identify, was hardly taller than myself. He toured me through the various departments and explained their history and function as we went. The tour took several hours and, when it was done, I was so tired and bored that I couldn't stifle a few wide yawns. As such, I was grateful when the proctor finally led me to the student's residences in a building which zigzagged down the beachfront so that each student had a private view of the ocean from his window. I was assigned to a large cubicle with private commode on the ground floor.

When I entered my quarters, the first thing I noticed was the wide projection screen covering one entire wall. The proctor explained that some subjects do not require a formal classroom structure and, as such, are simply projected onto the screen so students can relax and study in the privacy of their own rooms. Being somewhat reclusive by nature, I was delighted to receive this news. All the· walls of my large cubicle were painted white. On the wall opposite the screen there was a large table which held an appliance remotely resembling a computer of some kind, along with several other instruments whose name or function I could not begin to guess. The proctor told me another person would be along later to instruct me in the use of all equipment. But first, he said, he would leave me to get some rest.

Yes, I was tired. It had been a long day. But how could I sleep when faced with such an adventure? I couldn't wait to learn to use all the technology that this culture must possess. Instead, I looked for a latch so that I could open the patio doors to the outside. You can imagine my surprise when my hand went right through the pane! On closer inspection, it proved to be a sort of air-curtain which I could walk right through. Boy, they must have a lot of trouble with burglaries. Either that, or they operate on a fool-proof honor system! And I thought back to my old neighborhood and how this type of window would fail radically back there.

I stepped outside. Wide terraces ran the length of the building, with divider walls separating the lanais of each room. The walls were topped with planters from which spilled multicolored flowers of pink, blue, yellow and crimson. I took a deep breath. The air smelled very different from the air back home; it was saltier and had another quality which I couldn't identify. I walked to the beach and stood for a long time, looking at the ocean splashing the beach with regularity, admiring the panorama. I wondered who my neighbors were, as I hadn't seen another soul since my arrival at the residence, and concluded that classes must be in session at that time of day.

Returning to my quarters, I took a long, cool shower from an overhead spigot that rained on me the moment I stepped under it. Then I stretched out on the hammock-like apparatus that was slung along the wall and found that it adjusted to my contours in perfect comfort. I thought I'd have to count sheep or something, because I still felt too keyed up, but I was wrong. The minute I closed my eyes, I was asleep.

When I awoke, I knew something had changed. Either my own innate sixth sense or one of the new senses they had imbued me with on the ship was working overtime, sending off little alarms inside my head. Raising up on one elbow, I looked around suspiciously. Nothing was disturbed in the room, no one was in sight. Then what was causing these little shivers of warning to run up and down my spine? It was as if there was an alien spirit in the room with me, preparing to do mischief. I was unnerved and scared. To play for time, I pulled my glasses from my pocket and carefully polished them on the hem of my shirt. Then I placed them on my nose and examined the room again. Well, it might be invisible, but there is definitely something in here besides me, I thought.

"Who is here?" I called, a little too loudly. I was shaking like a leaf. Suddenly I wished I had not agreed to come to this place. My life at home on Terra may have been awful and the kids abusive, but at least I knew what I was dealing with and how to deal with it. Here, on planet Teenpon, I was out of my league and ill-equipped to handle myself against an invisible adversary.

"Speak. Who are you? Identify yourself," I commanded shakily.

Silence followed. Then there was a tingling inside my cerebral cortex and words noiselessly wrote themselves on the blackboard of my mind.

"Do not fear me," was the message.

"That's easy for you to say!" I retorted. A little anger was taking the place of fear. Maybe I couldn't see this thing, but I could communicate with it, and it had no right barging into my space like this.

"I am a being composed of pure energy, a step beyond light, many steps beyond sound. You cannot see me because there is nothing to see. I am not composed of matter, as I said, only of energy; therefore I have no substance " unless I inhabit and control something of substance. If you had a puppet, I could inhabit the doll and make it move and talk so you could focus on me, but you have nothing in this room that I can inhabit. "Wait! I have an idea!" The projection screen suddenly flickered on and a moving display of phosphorescent light could be seen.

"Here I am! I can make myself into a display of energy on your screen. Is that better?"

"I guess. But all I can see is bands of phosphorescent color. Do you have a form?"

"No. The problem with races composed of matter is that all they can relate to is other matter. I told you, I am pure energy. Try to comprehend this basic concept and we will get along just fine."

"Okay, but you'll have to give me some time. I'm not used to dealing with things or beings unseen, you know. On my planet, anything unseen is called a ghost or a poltergeist, or some other form of occult energy which makes us afraid."

"I understand. What do they call you on your planet?"

"David, and do you have a name, too?"

"Yes, but it would be impossible for you to say because it is composed purely of energy patterns and not sounds. You can call me Sparkie, though, if you like."

"Okay, Sparkie. Why have you come to visit me?"

"I am sent to be your friend, guide and guardian. Actually, I have been assigned."

I wasn't sure how I would go about being friend to an invisible entity, but I sensed I was expected to cooperate in every way. "Okay, I guess that will be fine." My answer was worth ten points for politeness and zero points for conviction.

How was I to guess from this meeting that Sparkie was to become my closest and most faithful friend and advisor, who would save my life more than once during the course of our friendship? After all these years, he still comes when I need him, the same supercharged Sparkie of old, for as you know, pure energy beings never age.

Later that day, I met Hella, who was destined to become another friend of mine. She appeared in the doorway of my room, tall and graceful, her entire body covered in bright coppery fur, which caused me to think of a squirrel, and regarded me quizzically with huge, beautiful golden eyes. Standing there like that, spread-legged, hands on hips, she looked aggressive and a bit arrogant. I felt clearly intimidated by her.

"Well! What have we here?" she barked, as she critically surveyed me from the top of my head to the tip of my toes. "Another freshman!" She laughed then, and entered my room with such a swift movement that I involuntarily jumped aside, for fear that we would collide.

"I have been sent to explain things to you," she

said, approaching the table on which all the equipment stood. "My name is Hella," she said over her shoulder, 'and I come from O'Bria in the farthest corner of this Galaxy. What do they call you?"

"D-d-d-d-david," I stammered.

"What is wrong with your speech unit?" she demanded.

"N-n-n-nothing," I stammered again. "I'm just nervous. I've never seen anything ... er ... anyone like you before," I was slowly regaining composture.

"Talking to a giant squirrel throws me a little off-balance."

"Giant what?" She either didn't understand me or took offense at the comparison.

"Nothing, never mind. Anyway, you don't look like a squirrel, just your color and your fur remind me... I'm sorry if I've annoyed you."

"There is a difference between puzzlement and annoyance, Daveed," she pronounced my name with awkwardness. "Now, shall we begin with Syntuxx?" She pointed to the screen which was connected to a wide keyboard having countless buttons and switches in many colors. "This will give you access to the memory bank, the library, and to the great Academic Computer. Sit here and I will show you how you can access the Academic Computer memory containing all of the history of our galaxy and what we have learned of the galaxies beyond."

She pressed a button and the computer lit up. Another, and the information on the screen showed the menu she had called up.

"Now, in order to call up any specific planet, you must keep narrowing your selection by first calling up the solar system, then the specific planet and period in universal time or reference to a specific date in that planet's recorded history. It's quite simple." She ran her fingers over the keyboard as though it was a musical instrument, as I watched, fascinated.

Once I've managed to overcome my fear of this lady, I noted that she was very beautiful, quick and graceful while possessing great strength. Before long, I was under Hella's spell as she explained the operation of the giant screen on my wall and several other things such as how to take a refreshing bath of negative ions, how to use the Memor-Tap, and how my hammock worked through the adjustment of powerful force bands. It was mind-blowing to try to assimilate all this information in one go, but she explained that all freshmen were ignorant of these things and I was no exception. She assured me it would all be second nature to me in no time at all.

Then she shook her thick coppery mane and said, "Come with me, Daveed, now I want you to meet Migo." Without further explanation, she walked through the air curtain and waited for me to follow. We walked among the campus buildings, between two huge pools which reflected blossoming trees on their mirrored surfaces. The flowers were shaped like bells and bright yellow in color, and on future days whenever there was a strong breeze, I thought I could hear them ringing faintly.

Hella was walking very fast and I had to hurry to keep up. By the time we arrived at our destination, I was plenty winded and staggered along behind her, gasping for breath.

We entered a strange-looking, low building constructed of irregular rocks. This building seemed out of place here in Teenpon. At first, I wondered why, and then I realized it was because it was the sort of a building I had seen back home in pictorial essays on Europe. Inside, it was very dark and cool, and at first I couldn't see a thing. Hella put a hand on my shoulder and guided me along.

Gradually, my eyes adjusted to the gloomy semi-darkness of the passageway and I thought I was in some kind of tavern. I turned to tell Hella that I was underage for such a place and that someone would no doubt be along any minute to throw me out, but at that moment she pushed me down into a low, plush seat and sank into an adjoining seat herself.

"Tell me what you want to drink," she said casually, looking around as if she expected to see someone she knew. I thought of a can of ice cold cherry Coke, and then remembered I was on Teenpon. There would be no cherry Coke here.

Suddenly Hella waved energetically at someone and within moments a creature approached our table and sunk into a seat on the opposite side.

"This is Migo," Hella presented her friend. The newcomer wasn't a pretty sight, and I was disappointed with his arrival. Fat and bloated, sporting a big stomach barely supported by spindly, short legs, he looked almost grotesquely comical. His face would have been ugly if it hadn't been for a pair of extraordinarily big, luminous eyes.

His ears were large and quivering and his skin was soft and pink, like a baby's, and nearly translucent.

I was to learn that Migo was a genius. There wasn't anything he didn't know about any subject in the universe. Now, his big eyes scanned me for a brief instant. Then he smiled, and I felt better; I felt accepted at once. A trolly rolled up to our table, full of glasses containing liquid in different colors. A metallic limb suddenly whirred out from the trolly and plucked a glass of refreshment from its top, setting it before me. I was very thirsty after my effort at keeping pace with Hella, and so glad to see a refreshment that I tipped it to my lips without stopping to guess what it was.

One sip caused me to drop my chin in astonishment. It was cherry Coke! Wow! Miracles never cease. I drained my glass in one pull and wished for a refill, then another.

Hella explained that the computer read my mind and blueprinted the flavor I desired, then synthesized it for me. She said it was no big deal, that I would get used to this type of service before long. Quite unexpectedly, many tiny points of light shimmered over our table, announcing the arrival of another friend whom I'd already met. It was Sparkie, of course.

I greeted him and turned to Hella. "What is this place called?" I asked my hostess.

"We call it The Pit," she replied. "It's the meeting place for all students, but mostly frequented by the rebels and enterprising thinkers among us. Here, the fate of the worlds is discussed, analyzed and resolved. Here you will meet new friends who will be your faithful lifetime companions."

In the course of that afternoon, I learned that pure energy beings like Sparkie were the most prolific life form in the universe. I learned that they inhabited Terra as well, and that the human race was almost completely ignorant that they shared the same plane of existence with them. I learned that Sparkie and his fellow beings were totally invisible except for rare moments when they experienced love and joy, and in those moments they would radiate colors.

"Have you ever seen a flash of light, like a firefly, moving with the speed of lightning, which caught your eye just off your peripheral plane, and if you quickly turned to look, there was nothing there?"

"Yes, many times. I remember I did."

"Well, whenever you see this phenomenon you can be sure that one of us is around and perhaps even trying to make contact with you, who knows? Many of my kind are destined as guides to the life forms which live in fleshy bodies, and whose vision is somewhat limited. But you must never be afraid," Sparkie said soothingly, "for we never mean to harm a living soul. Pure energy accompanies a pure thought, so relax!"

Eventually, Migo told me some of the secrets of the universe, and it made my head spin in wonderment. I became very fond of my friends; they were the only friends I ever had in my young life, except for Wang and Rex and Phaedra. And I was happy in the Academy, truly happy for the first time in my life.

Classes were not too difficult once I opened my mind completely to new dimensions of thought. Among my many subjects were Astronomy, Astronavigation, Philosophies of Time and Space, Harmony of Spheres, Cybernetics, Self Defense through the use of Mind power, and the Technology of Light. But the most challenging of these was the course on subatomic structure and synchronicity of the mind with subatomic particles.

Learning the mind-speech was easy, as were levitation and telekinesis, once we mastered the proper prana-otani breathing techniques and trance states. I had some difficulty with the class in Unconditional Love, though. For I could love almost any being, be it Reptilian, Canine or Lyrinx, but Furies? How can anyone love a Fury? Nevertheless we all had to learn to love every living, crawling, flying, swimming or walking creature in the universe, unconditionally.

It was difficult for me to free my personality from the prejudice and fear of that which is strange and unknown, to disregard the appearance and sometimes the smell in order to explore the being within. After intensive training, I finally passed the Unconditional Love test with flying colors.

My favorite subject was the sociological structure of the Universe, which showed the interrelation between widely differing species and races. And I came to love Space navigation, and Garro playing when I had a split. This was my favorite pastime, but not just reserved for when I met with friends; you can play Garro by yourself on the big screen although it isn't as much fun if you do it alone. All in all, I wasn't such a bad student.

On one bright, sunny day, the four of us hid away in The Pit to escape the heat of the sun at its zenith, 'stretching out comfortably around our favorite table to sip refreshments while Sparkie flitted in and out of our airspace.

"I really hope we will be permitted to take our tests together," said Hella. "The Herculean Tasks are difficult, and it's good to have a friend by your side, and also to protect your back at a time like that." She stretched her long legs out in front of her luxuriously.

Let me pause here to explain to the uninitiated. All students of the Academy, upon completion of their curriculum, must pass twelve tests of strength and wisdom. These tests are called The Twelve Tasks of Hercules. When I first heard the name, I was surprised that they had used the name of the mythological Terran hero. But then it was explained that Hercules had been an experiment of the Galactic council which did not yield the expected results. Then, when the new law was shortly thereafter introduced which prohibited interference with life forms on restricted planets, all further experimentation was promptly squelched.

"Perhaps we can obtain special permission to follow the same assignments for all twelve Tasks," said Migo. He was far and away the best student in the Academy and our professors often spoiled him by catering to his wishes against their better judgment.

"I wish I had an inkling of what awaits us," I ventured.

"What sort of Tasks will we be assigned to, and where?"

Nobody knew the answer to this. Tasks were assigned at random and in order of appearance. When you showed up, you were assigned the next test. Pure luck of the draw. This random selection was designed to give everybody a fair chance.

I took a sip of cherry Coke and thought, Life is good. Then I learned back in my seat and enjoyed the moment.

"Together, as usual," an unpleasant voice screeched over my shoulder so unexpectedly that I nearly jumped out of my seat. It was Elgin, the Sylvan who, together with his group of misfits, envied and hated us for being so relaxed and happy together. I knew of Elgin's quarrelsome nature, so typical of these forest creatures, and just ignored him, sipping away nonchalantly at my cherry Coke. But Elgin was in an especially irritable mood today and he wanted to argue. Above all, he was in no mood to be ignored, not at all.

"Hey, guys, I challenge you to race against me, but no Levit tricks! If you don't pick up the glove, I'll denounce you before the whole campus and you'll be laughed at until you die of shame. Ha! Ha! Ha!" Malignant lights danced in his round eyes. How this character had passed the Unconditional Love course I'll never know. He must have cheated somehow.

Hella surprised me by hissing and spitting at him, "Get lost, you miserable son of the forest. I bet you'll drop those smelly little pants of yours if you try to race against me, stinky! Come on, let's go, stinkeeee!"

It was true. Sylvans did smell very stinky. It was their weak point. But Elgin's face turned red with fury.

"You, you .... I'll show you," he threatened.

"Shut up and get ready to run, you stinker!" Hella cut him short. The Sylvan stamped his hooves in anger and frustration. "Stinker" was the most offensive thing you could call a Sylvan.

Now I noticed that Elgin's friends stood in a circle behind him. They were a collection of ruffians all born under different stars, and it looked like they were plotting some kind of action to provoke us. I decided to be the peacemaker and got out of my chair. However, they didn't listen, wouldn't let me say anything, wouldn't break their circle to let me in. Quite obviously, they wanted to fight and there was nothing I could do to stop them.

Both groups moved outside. There was an isolated spot some distance from the campus, on the plain of Leara, where we could settle our disagreement in privacy. We summoned a Tolux to take us there, and the flying taxi arrived at once. Jumping inside, we punched our course into the autopilot and dropped a token in the slot to cover the fare. Being wedged inside that cabin with Elgin and his cronies caught us in a whirlpool of negative energy which made my nose curl up in distaste and set my teeth on edge.

Being subjected to such physical discomfort was very distressing for me, and I found myself on the verge of tears from sheer repugnancy. So much for my conditioning in Unconditional Love, I thought, I'm no better than a Sylvan! My skin prickled and all the hairs stood on end, but I rolled my eyes up and forced myself to think of something else long enough to get through this ride.

Fifteen minutes later, we reached our destination and disembarked on a desolate plain covered with reddish dust and dotted with a few scattered boulders and not much else. A strong wind gusted across this open space occasionally, showering us with debris and filling our eyes, ears and clothing with dust. I made the mistake of licking my dusty lips and then had to contend with a mouthful of gritty particles sticking between my teeth.

Why in blazes did we come out here? I wondered at the stupidity of the situation. Why did Hella take up this idiotic challenge anyway?

But things were happening too fast now for me to intervene. Hella was psyching herself up and I could see that she was beyond reason. "I'll show these stinkers who's best and who isn't," she cried.

"Dave, I don't like this," Sparkie whispered in my mind.

"Me, neither," I replied. "But what can we do to deter them? They said, "No tricks. ""

"I have an idea," Sparkie responded, and I felt him depart.

What can he have in mind? I wondered.

Meanwhile, the preparations for the race were finished and Elgin and Hella stood on the starting line, elbow to elbow, ready for the signal to run.

The rest of us got back into the Tolux in order to watch their progress from the air. I wondered if Hella could really beat him? After all, Sylvans were purported to be the fastest creatures in the galaxy.

The race began. I knew Sparkie didn't enter the Tolux along with the rest of us, and supposed that he was roaming around down below somewhere near the runners. Observing the scene carefully, I was ready to command our taxi to descend immediately if Hella appeared to be in trouble. She was running well, so far, her head thrown back and red mane flowing behind her like the tail of a comet. A yard or two in front of her, Elgin ran in big, jerky jumps which covered several yards with each thrust.

"Oh, dear," I groaned. It looked like she didn't stand a chance.

"Have you seen Sparkie? I wonder what he's up to?" whispered Migo in my ear. He was standing just behind me, the sweat pearling on his baby-fine skin.

"I wish I knew," I replied.

The Sylvan was already five yards ahead of Hella and gaining more ground with every second. The terms of the race, as set forth by Elgin and his group, were murderous.

The two were to race until one of the opponents fell down exhausted and could run no more. This was unspeakably poor sportsmanship, but Hella agreed to it in defense of our honor.

Our opponents formed the majority in the taxi cabin, and they were having a great time, cheering their leader and simultaneously jeering at us spitefully. Their group contained two more Sylvans, plus a Fleex with shifty eyes and a shrewd expression on its foxy face, and one Gantee whose big, flattened head and watery eyes teetered precariously on its thin and spindly chicken legs. They were a rogue's gallery, if ever I saw one.

Down on the red desert plain, the Sylvan had distanced himself a good twenty yards in front of Hella. Suddenly he stopped, turned around, and made mocking faces at her, taunting and laughing at that brave girl. I saw his mouth move and felt certain that he was saying cruel things to her. It wasn't fair. When she was a yard away from him, he started running again, staying just out of her reach. I was getting angry. This had to be stopped before he ran Hella to death. I knew how proud she was; she would never give up, even if it cost her her life.

"What is Sparkie doing down there to help?" I wondered. "He said he had an idea!"

Suddenly, Elgin fell to the ground in mid-stride, to the utter astonishment of everyone in our cabin. I watched as he scrambled to his feet again, rubbing his eyes and choking on the red dust he must have swallowed. What was happening to him? Elgin looked to be as surprised at his fall as we were. He shook his head in disbelief and resumed, but with the difference that now he was scanning the ground suspiciously for potholes or stumbling blocks. This slowed his pace somewhat, and Hella gained on him a little as the race went on.

Then Elgin fell again, biting the dust as he had the first time. We cheered while Elgin's support group booed and whistled. Hella was clearly taking over. She was ahead now, waving her hands up at us triumphantly. Elgin got to his feet and shook his body violently to rid it of the dust, the surprise and anger visible on his face even from this distance.

He ran again, but this time his progress was much slower and more cautious than before. He almost seemed to hesitate before each jumping step as if to scan ahead for a sure-footed landing. When he fell for the third time, we took the Tolux down and touched ground next to him. He lay on the ground, unmoving.

Hella retraced her steps and reached us, breathing heavily. She smiled at us widely, almost at the end of her endurance, but her beautiful golden eyes shone with the excitement of victory. We turned Elgin face-up. He wasn't dead, just unconscious.

"Well, I guess we should declare ourselves the winners!" exclaimed Migo.

Elgin's group collected their leader from the ground and loaded him unceremoniously aboard the Tolux.

"What happened?" I asked Hella. "Did Sparkie have a hand in this?" She laughed. Little shimmers over her shoulder told me that Sparkie was here, too.

"We agreed not to do levitation tricks, remember?" she explained innocently. "But there was no rule about using illusions, was there?"

"No, there wasn't. And I forgot that Sparkie is a master of illusion." Sparkie spoke up.

"I simply created the illusion of a precipice in front of Elgin, and each time he fell, he believed he was falling into an abyss, when of course he only fell a few feet and kissed the ground." We all laughed, happy that the challenge had ended without anyone getting hurt.

The six years that I spent in the Academy were the happiest period of my life. Sometimes I thought about Mom and Dad, and sometimes I even dreamed about them. When I missed them, it made me sad, but those moments were really the only clouds on an otherwise unbroken string of sunny, carefree years on Teenpon.

CHAPTER 8

By the time I was eighteen, according to the Terran calendar, I had acquired all of the schooling needed preparatory to the Herculean Tasks. Somehow, my friends and I managed to convince the committee governing assignments to treat us as a team. As such, we were to be given group assignments for all twelve of the Herculean Tasks.

I was so excited over the challenge of confronting those tests that my expectations exceeded the fact and left me severely disappointed with the first three.

For the first Task, we drilled tunnels in the mountains of G'tir and regulated the climate of that ruggedly barren planet through the scientific redirection of its strong winds. This task was fairly elementary.

For the second Task, we were sent to explore one nearby virginal satellite body, chart it and return with maps showing the geological configuration as well as flora and fauna. It, too, was a fairly routine and boring exercise, because by pure luck of the draw, we got a desolate sphere with no life on it. Just the same the work had to be done and we did what we could with an uninspiring subject.

The third Task was somewhat more interesting: to protect the fragile inhabitants of the planet Caria against its harsh climate and diminishing energy from its blue sun, Loh. We built Caria an artificial sun to warm its frosty days, and seeded trees over the surface of the planet to provide a thick canopy to retain and improve the atmosphere. The inhabitants, gentle, high-vibrational beings, were so grateful and elated that they didn't know how to thank us enough.

CHAPTER 9

The fourth Task provided all the adventure I sought, and more. We were assigned to solve the mystery of the ancient Jappa. Because their planet was swampy, we spent some time searching for an appropriate landing spot. We flew as close to the ruins as we could, and finally succeeded in landing safely on a small, rocky bluff. The humidity of this area was such that the air was hard to breathe and was so heavy with moisture that we were bathed in sweat the whole time. Migo sweated the most profusely and suffered terribly because of his weight.

When we'd secured our ship, we began our journey to the ruins in a small amphibian vehicle called the FROG. Let me pause to explain that the mystery of the ruins of the ancient city of Kath lay in the fact that several expeditions had been sent to explore the remains of that once great civilization before us, but none of them had ever returned or even transmitted an electronic report back to the Academic Committee. We were thus well aware that we could lose our lives on this assignment and were fully prepared for danger on this mission. Yet the Council wanted the mystery solved and thought we were the best recruits for the job.

The cabin of the FROG was very small, and with Migo occupying at least half of the available space, we were very crowded. At any rate, I felt very cramped and claustrophobic. Soon, we arrived at the high stone wall which surrounded the city and towered over us like a menacing shadow.

"Hey, boys and girls, there are energy beings like me all over this place!" Sparkie chattered excitedly from his position, which was plastered to the roof of the cabin of the FROG.

"Good! Will they help us, do you think?" asked Hella, who was curled uncomfortably on her seat with her legs doubled up under her body.

"I can't say," Sparkie whispered, as though he were afraid they could hear. "I'm not sure of their dispositions. There are those who prefer to isolate themselves from any responsibility in regard to affairs of the galaxy or its inhabitants. They lead a self-sufficient and completely free and happy existence, far from any material concerns."

"Then why are you so different? Why did you join the Academy?" asked Migo, as he scrutinized the terrain on the photo screen in the console.

"I was bored, for one thing; longed for adventure and fun. Some of my pure energy companions live pretty dull lives in their isolation. And that's okay, if that's what they want. Me, I'm sociable, so I made an unusual choice and you see the result!"

"Well," I encouraged my friends. "Here we are together and no one will stop us from our appointed task, since freedom of choice is the first rule in our constitution: And ye shall do as ye wish and go where ye choose while no harm is brought to bear on another living thing by that action."

They joined me, reciting the merry chorus.

It became unbearably hot and stuffy in the cabin. Our atmosphere exchanger was working overtime, but to no avail. Migo pushed the transparent canopy open, but that only let in more of the wet blanket of air. It was oppressively hot outside, with not a hint of a breeze. Migo complained that he was being steam-cooked even as he sat.

After slowly passing through the high, arched stone entrance to the city, we navigated through marshy ground and the FROG sprayed muddy water on either side of us in a fan-shaped wake. The fog was forming in thick, milky patches now and it lent an unreal aspect to the scene, like something out of a dream. Hella shifted uneasily in her seat.

"I don't like this place," she said. Her eyes turned to dark amber, as they always did when she felt nervous and apprehensive.

"Hold onto your seats!" Migo stopped the vehicle with a jerk in order to avoid hitting an awful-looking, slimy green creature with countless tentacles, which stood right before us, waving agitatedly.

"Stop! Stop!" We all understood its cry. "Go no further. Turn back immediately!" warned the slimy thing.

"Why should we listen to you? What's ahead that you are compelled to warn us against?" Hella demanded haughtily.

"Explain yourself!"

The slimy green creature seemed to look around itself with its several dozen eyes, which were located in most unusual places. It waved its tentacles as if to punctuate its speech. "No! No, I can't tell you. Just turn back before it's too late," he cried out for the last time, and abruptly melted into one of the pools.

We stared at the surface of the water, transfixed, until the muddiness settled and we could see clearly to the bottom. Nothing was there, which left us all wondering whether we'd been subjected to mass hallucination. The event had clearly made us all nervous, so we adjusted the stun-guns on our belts before continuing. Council's policy was to preserve all life forms everywhere, despite any threat to the lives of explorers from our society. Our weapons were therefore incapable of doing more than stunning any aggressor, and promised little in the way of damage, outside of a lingering headache. Obviously, the objective in stunning an aggressor was to allow time for escape or retreat to safety. That is, assuming these options would be available.

Our FROG rolled forward more slowly under Migo's capable direction and soon we were passing structures that looked like the remains of fallen buildings, ruins with aged edges and slabs of stone that were pointing at the sky, having been dislocated by some long-ago quake. The components of the ruined structures were now covered with moss and other fungi which looked greyish and sickly.

I wiped my glasses for the umpteenth time, to remove the vapor of steam which covered them. They were fogging over nearly as quickly as I wiped them dry, and it was becoming harder and harder to see.

"Sparkie, could you fly ahead and scout the area for us?" asked Migo. "That way, if there is any real danger, you can detect it before we arrive and hurry back to prepare us. You can do that without risk of harm to yourself, can't you? Pure energy beings, like you, are indestructible, if I recall my cosmic biology correctly."

Migo was capable of recalling an entire encyclopedia correctly, so we let that one go. Sparkie flashed his record and left the FROG without a word. We slowed down, puttering along while we waited for Sparkie to return with a report on the conditions that lay ahead. Minutes passed in silence, but Sparkie did not return. We waited an hour. still no sign of our friend. That was when we really got nervous.

Finally I broke the silence.

"What could have happened to him? What could they possibly do to a being that can't be materially trapped, caught, held or destroyed, and who can pass through matter with ease." No one replied. Time dragged on and Sparkie didn't come back. Now we were beginning to feel guilty for sending him out there into danger; guilty, worried, and frightened at the same time.

We couldn't wait any longer and agreed tacitly

to venture forth and try to discover what had become of Sparkie. The FROG rolled along, splashing through the muck. The high canopy of the forest obscured the daylight and it became more and more difficult for our headlamps to pierce the gloom. Migo turned on our rotating searchlight and we could see that alien vegetation surrounded our trail. Everywhere there were thick vines and roots intertwining with the bricks of fallen structures. A lone bird sounded a cry of alarm somewhere high over our heads and I felt a chill despite the hot, thick, sticky air.

This place had a sense of evil foreboding about it, and fear was creeping through my veins, threatening to paralyze me. I could see that Hella and Migo were experiencing much the same sensation and had come to feel the same apprehension I did. Migo was sweating more profusely than ever and Hella's lower lip was involuntarily trembling.

Our vehicle moved forward slowly and cautiously, then suddenly it lost traction and we were floating -- no, we were sinking -- as the FROG's weight carried it downward.

Fortunately for all of us, Hella's reflexes were quick and she slammed and sealed the canopy shut before the water level reached the sill as we submerged. Then we were descending into a black and watery world populated by curious, shadowy shapes that gathered around us as we sank, bumping against our transparent canopy as though trying to get inside. My flesh was covered with goose-bumps and I was definitely petrified as we surged downward into the blackness. Now, through the canopy, I could see ghastly phosphorescent shapes closing in around us and heard Migo's involuntary, stifled gasp of terror. I would have cried out, too, had my vocal chords not been paralyzed with fear. The nightmarish, slithering things plastered themselves to the canopy and seemed to want to suck out our life energies.

Was it a hallucination, or was I weakening? I felt my thought process slowing down, felt the blood in my veins pumping sluggishly. Even my sense of fear had weakened; the adrenal in was not pumping now.

Abruptly, the whole scene vanished -- the water, the phosphorescence, everything -- just as if someone had opened a door and we'd fallen through. We were dropping through a colorless void, tumbling and spinning without control. Migo moaned painfully and Hella shrieked, while I held fast to my seat and hoped my restraints would hold in order to avoid being tossed about like my companions.

I sensed terror in this void, terror vibrating in every ion, drawing us into a vortex, spinning us towards its center. Our skins prickled and our body hair stood on end as though electrically charged.

Where are we? What are we falling toward? My mind was racing, but no reply came to my silent questions.

The emergency lights in our cabin cast a reddish glow on our pale, frightened faces. Hella's beautiful golden eyes were dark with fear and looked like two pools of molten lava.

Then we felt a tremendous pressure and heard the sound of our cabin being cracked open as if squeezed by a giant fist. Our windshield shattered into a zillion particles of plexi-glass and we automatically pulled on our support masks in anticipation of atmospheric suffocation. Clearly this invisible pressure was about to explode the FROG and crush us between its collapsing walls. What to do? We had to act, quickly!

Nothing occurred to me. I was too paralyzed with fear. My teeth clattered painfully and my body was streaming with sweat, causing the restraint straps to chafe cuttingly.

Meanwhile, the FROG kept turning and tumbling over and over through the blackness, the emergency lights illuminating big cracks and dents in its solid metal walls and floor. Flashes of malignant violet light burst through the blackness outside from time to time. Then the horrible sound of crushing steel almost deafened us, as our cabin collapsed around us. I hit my eject button and felt myself flying through the broken canopy opening just as the FROG burst into flames. Then I felt a terrible crushing pain and nothing more, as the void penetrated and absorbed me.

CHAPTER 10

When I woke, the crashing pain was still there, only worse than before, so much so that I almost regretted having regained consciousness. My head throbbed violently, and I had an awful taste in my mouth. I tried to move, and couldn't because something was holding me tight. I tried to relax and analyze the situation. My hands and legs weren't bound and yet I could not move.

Why? In spite of my excruciating pain, I opened my eyes. At first, I thought I had been blinded, for everything around me was pitch black, but after a few minutes my eyes adjusted to the dark and I could distinguish the strange shapes of alien objects beyond me somewhere. I also felt there was a denser ring of darkness outside my immediate reach, like a force field, which held me imprisoned. What I didn't know was that the force fields were spheres which floated all around me in the blackness, their density being many times that of the void they floated in. I sensed that I was not alone. Perhaps other prisoners out there were being held captive in the same way that I was, but who or what they were, I couldn't begin to guess.

Perhaps Migo and Hella are being held, too, I thought, and then a sudden flash of insight hit me. Perhaps Sparkie is being held this way, too! Aha! This was the one possibility that hadn't occurred to me. Even a pure energy being couldn't break through a force field. And suddenly I understood why all the other expeditions had disappeared without a trace. I lay, helplessly, trying to imagine how many other life forms were floating endlessly out there. I tried to imagine what "out there" really was. The effect of all this imagining was something like counting sheep, for in no time I fell fast asleep.

When I awoke again I felt a little better. The headache was almost gone and I could concentrate with more clarity. I examined the blackness around me. I could see a few more details now. All around me there was only a dark void, but outside my sphere were other global shapes faintly outlined like black against dark grey. Yes! Just as I thought! Strangely enough, I could breathe without difficulty.

After a few more minutes, I noticed that there was a definite order to this place, wherever it was. The little spherical cells, for according to my hypothesis, that is what these things were, were all orbiting around a big, black monstrosity which was the nucleus of its mock planetary system. I tried to count them; the little spheres of darkness were innumerable and held in fixed orbits by some unknown energy field. My skin prickled despite the fresh, comfortable climate in my sphere. I strained my eyes to look out at the nucleus and it seemed monstrous, powerful and terrifying. Black as it was, it hurt my eyes to gaze upon it. So I closed my eyes and extended my other senses to examine it, but recoiled in panic when my mind touched its sheer force.

What is this thing? Is it a black hole, a magnetic body, or worse? Somehow I knew it was worse, much worse. I wished my friends were in here with me. I extended my senses once again, to probe the other globes for familiar life forms or the distinctive brainwave patterns of Hella, Migo and Sparkie.

I found Migo first. He was breathing heavily. In situations such as this, my telepathic powers came in very handy.

"Hello, there, Migo! Are you all right?" I communicated soundlessly. He caught his breath and then sighed deeply with relief.

"Is it really you, Dave?" he cried. "I thought you were dead!"

"No, it's me. I'm okay," I interrupted him. "Have you run an analysis of this place yet?"

"Err, yes, but I don't understand it," he reluctantly admitted. "We've probably fallen into an alternate dimension. There must have been a door or a hole in the fabric of time there at the bottom of the lake, and we fell through it into this alternate, unfriendly, incomprehensible environment. This black nucleus in the center must be a strange life form within this realm. It gives me the creeps, I don't mind telling you." Migo's voice trembled and I sensed that he shivered violently.

"Any idea how to get out of these spherical things?" I was feeling frustrated now.

"I'm working on it," he replied. "Give me some time and check back with me later. Meanwhile, perhaps you can amuse yourself trying to locate Hella and Sparkie. I have a feeling they are in here somewhere."

"I'll try," I reassured him. "Get back with you later, then."

I scanned sphere after sphere to no avail. Each one had an aura of negative energy which discouraged me from making contact. Not that I couldn't communicate with anyone of them, if I wanted to, mind you. As a Yav-7.6, my telepathic ability extended to all life forms and all languages. But right then all my concern was to find Hella and Sparkie.

Then, success! I located Hella's presence. She was squirming and fighting to break out of her invisible energy bond. Her brave, restless spirit just wouldn't succumb to captivity. But beating against her force field was of no use. The more she fought, the more it tightened around her, and the more firmly it held her in its grip.

"Hella! Stop fighting against that thing. This is Dave! Conserve your energy." I could sense a sudden cessation to her movement. "Migo is trying to figure out how to escape, Hella. I'm sure he'll come up with something, but he needs more time." I tried to sound reassuring.

"Davee!" She was excited to have heard from me. "We'd better come up with something soon," she complained. "I'm suffering from claustrophobia in here!" Then, before I could reply, she changed the subject. "Have you located Sparkie yet?"

"Not yet, but Migo and I think he's in here, too. How about you?"

"One of these force fields could trap him, sure enough, Davee," she agreed. "Let me know as soon as you've found him. "

My senses departed her sphere and moved on, going from one to another, scanning and searching for my friend. Thus most were occupied, I spent a long time at it, and after examining several thousand spheres, I was beginning to feel hopeless and ready to give up when a joyous spark of light filled my mind.

I had found Sparkie! The rapport was instantaneous and exhilarating. Using my mind, I embraced him spiritually with joy and reassurance. He flickered under the gentle touch of my emotional response.

"Any idea who or what has imprisoned us, Sparkie?"

"Yes. It's a concentration of the highest frequency of negative energy, and it's very powerful, just like a pure energy being. But its energy is twisted and malignant. You know about polarities, Dave? Well, this entity is of a purely negative character, which dwells at the negative pole of all energy. I don't know what caused it to be. I'll have to observe and report on this later." At this point Sparkie paused and seemed unsure how to continue.

"I think it feeds on negative energies. You know: anger, fear, frustration, sadness.... But this is only a theory. I need to spend more time in observation in order to be sure," he concluded.

I withdrew. The rapport was broken and I felt my throat tighten. How could such entities exist in the universe? And why? What caused this anomaly in the polarity of living things? How could it be possible to shift toward the negative pole in such a manner? Feelings of sadness and defeat overwhelmed me. I felt my bonds tightening, or was it my imagination again? Well, there was nothing more I could do at the present, and I felt mentally strained from the long orbital search, and so I curled up and took a nap.

CHAPTER 11

It could have been minutes later, or even hours for all I knew, that I awakened. I dreamed that I was riding Phaedra again, her silky mane gently fluttering against my face as we galloped through emerald meadows on my home planet of Terra. When I awoke, I felt refreshed and rested. I was almost feeling good. My orb didn't hold me as tightly as before and my bonds were looser now.

This was curious, indeed. Was the force field operated by the big, black nucleus? Did I have any effect on it? No! How could that be? This thought was so far off the wall that I laughed out loud. But why not give it a try? How else should I occupy my time?

Remembering my mind control classes at the Academy, I began with the deep prana-otani breathing which placed me in a light trance state. When I felt centered, I concentrated on feeling anger. This wasn't too difficult, considering the circumstances. As I concentrated, I felt the force field tighten around me noticeably. I wondered if this was a coincidence.

I decided to try something else and switched to concentrating on feeling filled with love and joy. This took a little longer, because I had to draw from distant past memories. But once I was radiating love from my very core, the force field loosened and I felt almost free of my bonds. Could it be as simple as all this? I still had my doubts. I repeated the process over and over and over until I was convinced.

It really works! I felt like singing and dancing with glee. I had found the way to freedom! I could cast off my bonds and free myself, as could my friends and all the other prisoners, once I shared the secret with them. Who would have thought it could be this simple, as simple as erasing all the negativity from our beings, as simple as concentrating on feelings of pure love. But it made perfect sense. Universal law tells us that love conquers all, does it not?

I was so excited by my discovery that I almost missed the movement. One of the orbs from the adjoining tier suddenly left its place and drifted into the center. Blackness closed around it, swallowing it without a trace.

No! This is terrible! A wave of rage and panic swept through me, and my force field almost squeezed the life out of me with its sudden and violent grip. I had to warn my friends; there was no time to lose. My thoughts were feverish now. If we all oppose this enemy with every bit of love we can summon, can we kill it with kindness? What then?

Who knows? Maybe we can break free together. I had to act fast, and contact my friends.

Migo was surprised not to have come up with the obvious solution himself. Hella was enthusiastic and volunteered to contact as many of the other prisoners as she could in the time we had. The movement to rebel against the dark force had begun.

"Didn't I tell you it feeds on negativity?" Sparkie shimmered with gladness.

"I just observed that it actually absorbs one of the spheres from time to time," I announced. "There must be prisoners alive or dead inside the nucleus who have achieved a state of maximum negativity, for as long as there is a spark of positive feeling, it can't absorb you."

"Good thinking, but we should hurry to break free of this monster, anyway," Sparkie concluded.

We all set to work to make contact with as many of the beings in the spheres as we could. Contacting some was very easy, while others had achieved too high a negative charge to place them within our reach. Little by little we built a force ring of love around our jailor. The stronger our positive force grew, the smaller our opponent seemed to become. The blackness receded as we controlled our thoughts and feelings carefully and linked up in a positive way with our neighbors. Now there was no room for negativity in our minds.

And gradually the blackness shrunk from us until we were held very loosely by spheres of light grey.

Mentally, I reached out to embrace all the prisoners with a message of love, and I felt them do the same, felt tentacles, hands, paws, and many kinds of limbs linking us in a broad circle of love. This final link had a devastating effect upon our jailor, who now became our prisoner. We were squeezing it to death. It could not escape. Our force was omnipotent, as thousands of orbiting beings from all over the universe joined in a massive shout of joy and love.

The nucleus tried to hit back, tried to strike at us with violet lightning, which had lost its power. We pressed forward. It shrunk from our love, shrunk into the size of an asteroid, then smaller and smaller until it was the size of a blimp, then a weather balloon, then a toy balloon, then ... pop! It flickered and disappeared. The space inside our circle was filled with sunlight and joy and our grey force spheres lost their power and were gone. What's more, we were all standing on the surface of the planet again.

We cried, we laughed and embraced and celebrated our freedom according to the customs of thousands of different solar systems, and our celebrating went on for many days and nights.

Thus was our fourth Task completed and the secret of the ancient ruins of Jappa solved. We learned that all the inhabitants of Jappa had been driven into the lake by an invading tribe. There they had fallen into the parallel world and had been imprisoned in the force spheres just as we were.

After returning to our ship, we decided to reward ourselves with a holiday on the pleasure planet of Snauru before returning to Teenpon for the fifth of our Herculean Tasks. Migo was the instigator of the holiday idea; he was determined to lose some weight before we embarked on any more adventures and Snauru was the place to do it pleasurably. So Hella, Sparkie and I decided to tag along. What the heck, we all deserved a break!

CHAPTER 12

For our fifth Herculean Task, we helped the inhabitants of the Odan system to fight the Grey Plague. It was no big deal. Neither was our sixth Task, which was to neutralize the bloodthirsty, birdlike creatures infesting the fifth planet of the Tantrax system. All intelligent life forms on that planet had been forced to retreat and live on the floor of the oceans from fear of being butchered by the aggressive, winged predators that soared tirelessly over the planet in search of prey. Since our galactic law forbids us to kill, we simply caught the vultures one by one and switched around the neutrons in their brains, forever erasing the aggressive tendencies from their natures. After that there were no more incidents on that planet. The predator birds, which had been feared for several hundred standard years, then retreated to live peacefully in the mountains while the inhabitants gradually took up their old agricultural pursuits on the planet's surface, never again to register a complaint.

On the seventh Task, I lost my glasses and

nearly lost my life as well. Dido, the planet to which we were assigned, was situated in the star system Atami in the most remote corner of the Siph nebula. It was rumored that Princess Liss o'Diss and the sacred Loxie stones of O'Venti were hidden there, but nobody really knew for sure. The kidnapping of the princess and the theft of the famous sacred stones of O'Venti had occurred sometime in the past and the event was famed throughout this part of the universe. Because our team had done so well on our previous assignment, the Committee decided to let us give it a try.

The intergalactic police had been hot on the trail of the princess for many years, using sophisticated detection equipment. But I looked forward to solving this crime because I had heard that Princess Liss o'Diss was of humanoid genetic component and very attractive at that. Furthermore, she was approximately my own age in Terran years, to judge by the holograms I later viewed. When I play them now, for old times' sake, her delicate, radiant face and large, luminous eyes still seem to look into my soul and my heart pounds like a sensual jungle drum.

CHAPTER 13

Since the Seventh Task was one of our more memorable adventures, I will give you a full account of it. While we orbited Dido, scanning the rugged surface, we tried to guess where our sought-after prize was hidden. Mostly, the surface of the planet was covered with the wildest ranges of mountains I had ever seen, topped by a thick layer of grey-white clouds, while the ground temperature registered as balmy and humid.

Obviously, finding the princess wasn't going to be easy. The deep canyons looked impenetrable, as though challenging anyone to dare to venture into their foreboding depths. Our life-scan sensors were useless here, for there was such an abundance of fauna that the entire planet registered as one huge organism pulsating with vitality. The mountain ranges were blanketed with lush forested vegetation in every imaginable shade of green.

We descended and entered the atmosphere. Hella and Migo peered at the screen, searching for a potential landing spot. Finally, they found it and our ship set down on top of a vast mesa.

When the last of our remote probes was completed and we received the computer's all clear to disembark, we opened the hatch and emerged, armed to the teeth with stun-guns and wearing our lightweight protective suits. Our tests had clearly indicated a C03 atmosphere which was breathable but ultra-loaded with oxygen which, after a few inhalations, had us feeling quite pleasantly high.

"Never thought a guy could get high on air alone," joked Migo.

"Perhaps we should propose to the Committee that they re-designate Dido into a pleasure planet," added Hella.

We were interrupted with a welcoming cacophony of sound. The breeze carried the cries and groans, hoots and howls, of all kinds of creatures, to our ears. Our historical reference material hadn't mentioned the presence of evolved intelligence on Dido, but that didn't mean there weren't a great many life forms having a social structure. Actually, I had the feeling that early expeditions sent to chart the system and study its life forms had done a pretty superficial job. I was prepared for anything.

"Hey, this isn't bad!" exclaimed Hella as she stretched luxuriously in the warming rays of the sun. "It's very like my home planet, O'Bria." A note of nostalgia was in her voice.

"So far, it is very pleasant, yes," agreed Migo, inhaling deeply of the fragrant herb-scented air. Migo, who had lost twenty pounds of body fat on our Snaura vacation, looked much more agreeable and was very proud of his trim figure. Sparkie hovered overhead, examining his new surroundings without comment.

"Wait!" exclaimed Hella. "I sense something. As if .. as if .. oh, I can't explain it, but there is something here we had better check out. Something that we wouldn't want to take us by surprise because by then it might be too late."

"When we scout the terrain we might be able to find the cause of this disturbance to your psyche or something might occur that would aid you to be more specific. Meanwhile, we'll be careful," Migo patted Hella's shoulder reassuringly.

"I'll scout! Scouting is my specialty," shimmered Sparkie.

"Yeah? Well, don't forget what happened on Jappa! You scouted yourself into a parallel dimension from which you couldn't escape."

Migo's friendly sarcasm was too much for the pure energy being who flashed a telepathic, "See you later," and took off for distant peaks.

Suddenly, I felt hungry, and said so. As it turned out, I wasn't the only one. Hella and Migo's stomachs were growling, too. So we got out our food supplies and sat on the grassy ground as if we were at a picnic, chewing our concentrated food cubes which tasted delicious when washed down with a bottle of teenberry wine that Migo smuggled aboard.

"Take it easy, Migo," laughed Hella as she gave her friend a gentle shove. "Leave some of that wine for the rest of us, or we'll put you on report for smuggling contraband aboard our mission, won't we, Davee?"

Migo sighed heavily and passed the flask to Hella. I hated to be another one to get on Migo's case, but I had been watching him gobble up food cubes as though they were in unlimited supply.

"Never mind the wine, buddy, I just wonder if you've noticed how many food cubes you've been putting away. Better save some for tomorrow, don't you think?"

Migo stopped midway to his mouth with another cube, looked guilty and hastily tucked it away.

"I'm supposed to be a genius, so why can't I figure out a way to eat as much as I like without getting fat? Huh?" he complained. "What's all this wisdom worth if I can't conquer this one simple problem?"

"Obviously the problem is not simple, if it has you stumped," contradicted Hella. "But think positive, Migo. You know, the old mind-over-matter philosophy; try that."

"You mean, I should get my mind to fool my stomach into thinking it's full when it's empty?" Migo suggested. "Do you really think that would help?"

Just then the loud buzzing of insects interrupted our conversation. I looked in the direction of the sound and saw that Migo's open container of food cube was crawling with bugs, while others were hungrily attacking the crumbs which had fallen on our suits. In fact, they were becoming quite aggressive, biting Migo's suit as he tried to shoo them away and close his food container.

"So much for picnicking in this place,"

complained Hella. "Looks like we'd better treat our dining as an on-board event from now on." We retreated to the ship and put away our food.

Half an hour later, Sparkie returned from his reconnaissance trip to report a huge canyon which traversed the planet, almost dividing it in two, as if something had occurred to split Dido open during the time of its early geological formation. He reported a canyon thousands of feet deep and covered with thick, impenetrable forestation on its slopes. At the bottom, he described a ribbon of thick, molten lava which flowed like a river in some places and a trickle in others. He estimated temperatures of more than two thousand degrees where the lava river flowed.

Above, in the mountain valleys, he reported an exceptionally high concentration of life forms, including huge predator birds which soared on the air currents looking for carrion.

"I felt glad not to have a material body," gasped Sparkie, "because they looked ready to prey on anything that moved. But I haven't told you the most important part. I sensed the presence of the Loxie stones of O'Venti, deep in the northern zone of the canyon. I could feel their power quite distinctly, and that means the stolen treasure is hidden there, too, or at least some part of it is," he concluded.

"Shall we fly there and take a look?" I questioned eagerly.

"That would seem to be the indicated action," Hella supported.

"All right. We'll wear our Gravi-T-belts and

secure the ship before we head out to investigate the area," Migo declared.

Minutes later, we were on our way. If you've never tried flying, in one of our Gravi-T-belts, you're in for a treat the day you do, believe me. The operation is simple; just push a button and you'll take off effortlessly. It's great fun. In fact, I almost forgot how serious our mission was because I was enjoying myself so much. I really got into the act of flying, soaring over peaks and forests as easily as a bird.

Sparkie guided us to the canyon and when I beheld the grandeur of it, I thought my heart would stop. Then it began pounding with excitement. I wondered if the princess could be somewhere down there, too. In my thoughts I called her my princess, and I was glad my friends were some distance from me and busy with their own thoughts so they couldn't read mine, or see me blush.

From this altitude the panorama was breathtaking, and as I looked down, I thought I saw movement between the trees and wondered what life forms lived there. Then I caught sight of the huge predator birds Sparkie had told us about. They looked more like pterodactyls than birds, if my memory of long ago Terran history books served me well. Actually, they gave me the creeps and I felt the hair rising on my neck as I watched them circle.

Just then I caught Migo's eye and jerked my head away from the birds to indicate that we should move out of their territory. Migo didn't have to say anything; he was sweating profusely again, as he always did when he was afraid. Hella's red fur was raised and her back was arched like that of an angry cat. Obviously she was intimidated by them, too.

"Is there any way to reach our objective while at the same time avoiding a confrontation with those things, Sparkie?" asked Migo urgently. Hella shuddered.

"I wouldn't like to go anywhere near those claws," she said in a small voice.

"Well, from what I can judge, these birds are the kings of the air here on Dido. So either you land and walk or make yourselves invisible like me. Although, if you land and walk, you don't know what predators you may encounter on the planet's surface. Also, I should warn you that walking through that rugged terrain would be dangerous and time consuming." Sparkie lapsed into silence.

"Ho! Well, thank you, Mister Sparkie, for your truly redundant and contradictory advice," Migo scoffed, then his voice took on a note of practicality as he continued. "As I see it, we would do best to return to the ship and use it to travel to North Canyon, as it shall be known. For without the ship's hull between us and those birds, for protection, I'd venture a guess that we don't stand a chance in the skies of Dido."

"Wait, Migo. How about if we drop altitude and swoop over the canopy of trees so we can land in the branches any time we need to seek refuge?" Hella ventured bravely.

"Besides, we are armed with our stun-guns after all." It was typical of Hella to choose fight over flight, and simply confront the danger. Migo was intimidated in the face of her bravery.

"Okay by me," he said with false enthusiasm. "What do you have to say about it, Dave?"

"Two out of three, I'm overruled anyway, so let's go!"

I alibied hastily before they could discover the truth. At that moment I felt I had a bright yellow stripe down my back. Deactivating the gravity fields which sustained our altitudes, we dropped like three stones and leveled off just above the treetops. Down here the air smelled of fragrant herbs, bittersweet fruit and rotting vegetation. Small birds and animals, living in the branches below us, ran in fear to hide away among the trunks, thinking us to be predators. Nearing the edge of the canyon, we could see the big birds circling high overhead and knew we had to be extremely careful. Descending even more, we flew beneath the canopy, and in so doing, got our first real close-up look at the vegetation. Those trees had been standing since the beginning of time and their trunks were thick and knotted.

I caught a movement on the ground, out of the corner of my eye, but when I turned my head to look at it, there was nothing there. That's odd, I thought. My eyes must be playing tricks on me today. Could have sworn something big moved down there through the underbrush a few seconds ago.

Again and again it happened. I would catch a movement just outside my peripheral vision and turn to find nothing at all. It was unnerving. And it was not my imagination! I began to feel uncomfortable and all my senses were on the alert.

There! It happened again! This time I noticed a long shape with a bright zigzag pattern on its back. It moved with the speed of lightning; no wonder I hadn't caught sight of it before! I couldn't exactly make out the shape of the creature and neither could Hella nor Migo, who had seen it too.

"Can you check it out for us, Sparkie?" I asked. "What kind of creature is that down there?"

"Whatever would you guys do without me?" he teased, as he winked away. Minutes later he returned, but he wasn't jolly anymore; he seemed troubled. We could feel him hovering above us in an undecided manner.

"Well, what is it, Sparkie? Are you uncertain how to identify the life form we saw?" Hella finally demanded.

"No ... " replied Sparkie thoughtfully. "It is a giant, carnivorous snake. There are so many of them down there that the sight of them fairly overwhelmed me. I have been trying to decide how to tell you without unduly alarming you."

"Gee. The missing element. Snakes on the ground and predatory birds in the air," grumbled Migo. "We have literally nowhere to go except where we are. Makes me wish we were back inside the ship."

At the edge of North Canyon, the view spread out before our wondering eyes in breathtaking splendor. I gasped at the magnitude of this geological marvel. The canyon was so wide that we could barely see the other side of it. Its banks descended in steep terraces, broken by areas of sheer rock face for thousands of feet. And down in the center of its depths could be seen an irregular thin line of bright red.

"There it is, the river of lava," whispered Hella in awe.

It was very hot, even at this altitude. My glasses were fogging over with vapor again, but at least this time I had remembered to bring my anti-fog spray. Sparkie directed us to the area where he had sensed the Loxie Stones deep in the bosom of the mountain. We were flying now in the canyon's deep shadow, the vultures soaring high above us and pacing us as we flew. Northward we flew at top speed until Sparkie circled and stopped.

"Here's the place. The Loxie stones are somewhere below. "

I could sense them, too. A strange, throbbing life force sending out its vibrations, which were not at all unpleasant. In fact, it was sort of alluring and magnetic. Since the Loxie stones are full of life, being sentient and bearing extensive knowledge in all fields, it is not surprising that they should be so valuable. The stones could answer any question put to them, no matter how difficult, providing you knew how to establish direct rapport.

Their font of knowledge made them rare in all the universe, priceless treasures which would bring the highest fame and lifelong esteem for those who engineered their recovery. I felt my heart beat a little faster now that we knew they were here.

Is Princess Liss o'Diss here, too? I scanned the visible portion of the gorge as if seeking the answer there. There were many terraces to be seen, some with dark openings which would lead into caves and possibly underground tunnels, unless my eyes were deceiving me.

"Hey, guys, I'll bet the treasure is hidden in the caves, but what of the princess?" I exclaimed. I sent my mind out to examine what lay ahead, invisible to us, hidden under layers of stone, and almost yelled out when I sensed a group of highly evolved beings, some of them almost humanoid, in the long tunnels leading out of the caves. I sensed a complicated network of passages leading to the heart of the mountain.

My boyhood love of adventure was never far away. Gosh, I'd like to explore them, I thought wistfully. I counted about a dozen intelligent life forms down there. All of them were in a group except for one who stood apart. My attention focused on the isolated one and I made a careful examination of its brainwave patterns. Yes! I was sure of it; it was the princess! The others were either her kidnappers or guardians, I decided.

I shared this discovery with my friends. We were all very excited. After all, we'd managed to locate our goal whereas all other search parties had failed. All we had to do now was to get the princess out of there together with the treasured stones, disarm her captors, and take them back to be put on trial. Hmmm, not an easy task. I sighed heavily. This would be difficult, at best, and very likely impossible.

So exhilarated were we with this discovery that we didn't notice the dark shadow which covered us. A flock of the predator birds had descended and were bearing down, claws at the ready, beaks extended, open and lined with sharp little teeth. Obviously, they were getting ready to snatch and devour us for lunch. Hella gave a little war cry and drew her stun-gun, which she began to fire full-force at our attackers.

Unfortunately, these weapons were never designed to kill and are not effective unless used at point-blank range. Their purpose is to disarm, disorient and disable the opponent, and no more. The predator birds were disoriented, at first, by the strange force of the stun-guns, but they had no intention of abandoning their hunt. One sharp talon passed dangerously close to my head, and another bird managed to catch Migo by one of his skinny legs and was towing him away. Migo yelled out in desperation and the bird gave him a violent jerk, tearing his suit and opening up a section of his leg. Migo yelled louder than before and Hella lost no time going to his rescue. Giving a bloodcurdling war cry, she aimed her weapon at the bird's head and hit it full charge. The bird swayed and unwillingly released its victim as it flew away, shaken and blinking its round eyes in disbelief.

I hardly saw what was happening, so busy was I fighting off two of the feathered menaces who were determined to share me for lunch.

"Flee, David, flee! More birds are coming!" Sparkie's warning cut through my own thoughts.

"Hella! Migo! Sparkie says we'd better get out of here. The rest of the flock is on the way here. They must have smelled Migo's blood!" As I hollered, I flew over and grabbed Hella with one hand and Migo with the other. Then, giving them the signal, I pushed my navigational button to descend and hit the accelerator at the same time, as we dove for cover under the canopy.

Because the birds were too big and awkward to fly beneath the canopy of the forest, we managed to defeat their attack and stayed under cover, mindful of the snakes, until they departed to hunt elsewhere. Whereupon we zoomed back to our ship, the trees now below us again and racing past us in a green blur. We must have set the speed record that day for Gravi-T-belts, I swear!

When we had finally reentered our ship and made it secure, we were totally exhausted.

Hella and I were fortunate to have survived the day's adventure with only a few bruises and scratches, but poor Migo's skinny leg was in poor shape indeed. Gently, Hella set Migo in the sonic bath and then handed him a fluffy robe to wear while she took a look at the wound. It was pretty ugly, all right. "This will require an application of Unibac and an hour under the Hypno-cure machine. That will fix you up, and you'll be good as new."

By the next day, there was not a trace of Migo's injury. But in the meantime, we were all due for a good rest.

CHAPTER 14

The next day was inactive but not unproductive. We sat around our ship's lounge and tried out various plans of action on each other.

"Did our research offer any information regarding who the kidnappers might have been?" asked Hella, as she stifled a yawn.

"Rumor has it that the kidnapping and theft were arranged by the House of Kirin, specifically spearheaded by Prince Arcobatt Kirin, sworn enemy of the House of o'Dissa," said Migo, delving into his encyclopedic store of knowledge.

"The feud between these two noble houses has lasted for several centuries now. One will do anything to spite the other. There is a substantial reward for whoever finds the princess and the treasure, you know," he added.

"Reward? We're not in this for the reward. The Task has been assigned, and I'm certain that would supercede any reward as far as we're concerned," I suggested, being the practical young man that I was then.

"Well, I think the reward will stand," said Hella,

"And I have a feeling we'll have it in our pockets before too long." She looked up slyly from the polish job she was doing on her nails and winked at me with one great golden eye.

"I hope you're right," I replied. "It won't be very easy with these pesky birds and snakes and whatever else we haven't encountered yet," I sighed.

"You know," Hella added, "the reward money is very considerable. On it, we could easily live in Snauru for the rest of our lives, just having fun."

"Never mind that," snapped Migo irritably. "I propose we fly the ship over and land on one of the terraces tomorrow. Do you all agree?"

We did.

CHAPTER 15

We started out at the first light of dawn. Our flight was short and uneventful, as was our landing on the terrace to one of the larger cave openings. The predator birds maintained a cautious distance from our disc-shaped craft and showed no signs of wanting to follow us. After disembarking, we activated the force shield which would secure the ship against all would-be intruders, adjusted our stun-guns and moved into the cave.

The floor of the cave was humid and slippery and there was no outlet. We emerged and, with the use of our Gravi-T-belts, jumped to the next terrace above and discovered there were caves with tunnels leading back into the mountain. There were seven caves and seven tunnels, no less, and perhaps even more were hidden from our eyes by the thick vegetation.

"Well, we found enough tunnels to satisfy anybody! Now, which one is the right one?" asked Hella impudently.

"Sparkie, you strike me as just the right one to find out," suggested Migo. So, while our invisible friend dashed off on his investigative mission, we three material beings made our way slowly toward the gaping cave openings.

I was so excited and nervous, I could feel the adrenaline cursing through my veins. To think that today might be the day I would come face to face with the vision in the hologram! To think I was actually going to meet Princess Liss o'Diss in person! My heart did loops and twirls every time I thought of her.

The chain of caves was right ahead of us now. Too impatient to wait for Sparkie, I projected my senses to scan the tunnels and perhaps find some indication of which was the right one. The strong throbbing in the life force caused by the Loxie Stones confused and distracted me, but I tried to ignore it and continued my scan. It was no good; the vibration was so powerful I couldn't tell which tunnel it was coming from and could not separate it from the other impressions I was receiving.

It was unfortunate that my telepathic powers were nullified by the force of the Loxie stones, and I thanked the muses for dear little Sparkie, who returned just then. It was a troubled Sparkie who told us that the complexity of the system of tunnels ahead of us could only be construed as a maze, and that we should mark our way as we progressed to avoid confusion or worse when we attempted to leave.

"Even with our sophisticated cybernetic search-scan equipment?" Hella asked in disbelief. "How could we possibly get lost with our omni-directional homing devices on our belts?"

"Just so," said Sparkie. "The stones are very strong and could cause equipment to fail." Of course, he proved right. He informed us, too, that the princess was being held deep in the center of the maze which reached the core of the mountain, and that she was asleep, imprisoned securely by a triple ring of Sylix and guarded closely at all times.

At the entrance, we paused, silently reciting to ourselves our positive affirmations against fear and programming ourselves mentally for action.

"Ready? Let's go, then!" Migo wiped the sweat from his forehead and led the way. We entered the tunnels and found that visibility was poor because very little light entered there. We didn't have to worry for long, though, since Sparkie simply shifted his consciousness and turned his energy field into a globe of light which led the way, illuminating us with eerie silvery radiance. The air in the tunnel was becoming heavy and smelled of dampness and rotting things. water dripped somewhere against stone ahead of us. But other than that, it was silent except for the sound of our own footsteps.

Hella walked ahead now, which was usual for her, as she was the least fearful of the three. The passage grew narrow and we walked single file. Our tunnel opened into other passages every so often and they branched off left and right. At every junction, we marked our direction with a phosphorescent green crayon arrow. After two hours, we stopped to rest and eat a quick meal.

"How much farther is it from here to the place where is the princess being held?" I asked Sparkie.

"We're halfway there."

"So far, so good, but we should beware of security surprises here," warned Migo, speaking more to himself than to us.

"Migo's right," Hella said. "Things are going just a little too smoothly, and this makes me suspicious.. I suggest we don't get too smug about this and drop our guard."

The mushroom concentrate which I loved now tasted bitter in my mouth. I guess I was nervous. The throbbing of the Stones was driving me bananas, and I knew the Loxie Stones were not too far away. I noticed a strange phosphorescent moss growing on the walls and watched it as I chewed on my food. It seemed to me that it shifted slightly. I thought I must be imagining things and tried to put it out of my mind. Hella handed me a canteen and I took a deep gulp. The liquid was warm and tasted sweet. I looked at the moss again.

Definitely, it had changed its pattern. I shared this discovery with my friends, but couldn't raise much interest in the phenomenon. I guess they had other things on their minds.

We finished our meal and moved on. The passage was narrowing and moving downhill. Hella, the tallest of our group, had to duck her head in order not to bang it against the low rocky ceiling. The air was becoming more dense, and we breathed it with difficulty. I was becoming claustrophobic; I never felt comfortable in tight places.

The throbbing of the stones was so strong now that I couldn't focus my thoughts. It was so disturbing that I wondered if it would drive me mad. I tried some prana-otani breathing exercises and mind control techniques, and that helped a little. We crawled around the 90-degree turn of our passage made in the rock and came smack up against a huge boulder blocking the passageway before us.

"What in a hundred stinking Sylvans is that doing there?" swore Hella irritably. Then she straightened up as the ceiling was higher here and examined the boulder thoughtfully.

"It's been put there on purpose," she announced. "But there must be a way to move it somehow. I'll bet there's a secret lock or lever that will trigger the opening mechanism." She ran her hands around the boulder, probed the walls, applying gentle pressure here and there, but after ten minutes of fruitless exploration she gave up.

"Well, Migo, we need your genius here," she said resignedly.

"David is the one who is force-sensitive here," he shrugged.

"Okay, let me see what I can do," I replied.

I sat on the cold, rock floor, crossed my legs and went into a trance with my hands on the boulder. Mentally, I scanned the interior of the stone and the tunnel walls around it. I detected no physical mechanism. There must be something else then, I thought. But, what? I tried to heighten my perception to its maximum reach, going into a still deeper trance.

And then I found it! In the very core of the boulder, I found it. A supersensitive cell conditioned to swing the stone aside upon impulse. But who could transmit such an impulse? And then in a flash, I understood the complete structure of the mechanism and how it worked. But I was so caught up in the trance that I saw more. I saw a hairless, gruesome entity bent over the long table where the Loxie stones lay, placing each stone in a separate compartment. The stones gleamed with a beautiful, inner golden light. The entity had given an order to one of the Loxie stones to send an impulse to activate the cell which controlled the boulder.

Well, then, and what if I were to communicate telepathically with that stone, and give it another order to slide the boulder aside? Briefly, as I speculated on this possibility, I scanned the other stones. No, this was the right one. Good!

Focusing my attention on it, I made my request. The stone which was keyed to the boulder was larger than the others, and it glowed with a golden light so bright it was blinding.

After a minute or two, I'm not certain how long it was, I felt the alien consciousness responding. I had greeted the stone as politely as I could and had made my request to be given access to the cell which would move the boulder. I had repeated the request several times, since I wasn't sure if the stone understood me. The consciousness seemed to hesitate, and I wondered if there was some secret access code that I should have used to identify my communication with. This troubled me, but I would never know for sure. Without warning, a searing white fire ripped through my brain and, blessedly, I fainted.

CHAPTER 16

When I came around, someone was hugging me gently. The soft fur and long, muscled arms told me it was Hella. She was singing a strange, exotic song in her low, melodic voice as she rocked me like a child. It felt good, and I was reluctant to open my eyes, but eventually I did. The first thing I saw was that the boulder blocking the passage was pivoted so that we could pass through.

Hella, noticing my state of awareness, took my head in her hands and pressed slender fingers to my temples as she probed my brain with her mind, searching for damage inside. Hella had studied psychic medicine for several years at the Academy and was considered an expert in her field. She must have been satisfied with her examination, because she let go and relaxed her worried face into a smile.

"Davee, you are one lucky guy!" she informed me. "No damage, just shock. Didn't anyone ever tell you the Loxie Stones can kill you if you attempt manipulation when your brain is not keyed to their vibrations or if you do not have proper training, even if your brain is keyed," she scolded. Seeing the troubled expression on my face, she smiled again.

"Never mind about that. You did it!" she cried, hugging me again.

"Hey, hey! This is no time for touching scenes of loving melodrama," growled Migo. "We must be on our way. Sparkie has already preceded us to check things out. Let's go!" There was irritation in Migo's voice. I wondered why Migo was so annoyed.

"Well, you certainly turned grouchy," snapped Hella.

"I've got a feeling you're jealous, and such feelings are unworthy of a genius!"

Migo reddened and turned away. I guessed Hella had hit a raw nerve. But there was no time to dwell on this development, for Migo had stepped past the boulder and vanished down the tunnel. Quickly we stood up and followed him. Hella remained behind me, supportively. We were now using the small halogen lights on our belt buckles to illuminate our way.

I locked my mini tractor beam in my chronometer onto the wave pattern of the Loxie stones, so we wouldn't get lost. The tracking mechanism would alert me with a beep if we went off course. We walked as quickly as we could, with Migo ahead and Hella bringing up the rear. I quickened my step until I caught up with Migo. I knew my friend was suffering the sting of embarrassment, but I didn't know what to say.

Then Hella caught up with us and put her arm across Migo's shoulder.

"I'm sorry, Migo, I was only teasing," she

apologized, and kissed him on the cheek. "I didn't mean to upset you, I was just so worried about Davee that I got carried away."

"Okay," Migo replied. "No hard feelings." We all joined hands and walked forward together. The ground was uneven beneath our feet now. There were potholes and cracks in the rock, and we became very careful where we stepped. Some of the holes were so deep we could not see the bottom. I wondered if these were booby traps. Anyway, no matter how careful you are, there is always something you might overlook.

That was the case with Migo. Suddenly, he stumbled and his legs disappeared into a hole up to his knee. He cried out in alarm and we were both at his side in a flash. We tried pulling him free, but it wasn't easy; his foot seemed to be caught.

"What is it? What's wrong?" I asked, seeing the look of panic on my friends' faces.

"What is it?" Hella shook Migo; his face was pale and frightened now.

"It's .. it's ..." He was too scared to speak.

"What?" Hella fairly shrieked.

"A ssssnake .... I think," he stammered. We all fell silent. "A bbbbbig one," he added after a while. "The more I pull, the tighter it grips me. I'm afraid it's going to crush my leg! Oh!" A grimace of pain distorted his placid face.

At this very moment, Sparkie zoomed out of the dark corridor ahead and circled over our heads.

"They are coming, they know we are here and they will kill you," Sparkie flashed.

"Cool down, Sparkie," growled Hella. "You are

safe and can complete the mission even if we die. But who are they? How many of them?"

Migo said nothing, he just looked at me and winced with pain.

"They are coming!" Sparkie insisted. "All of them! Five Broomaks, three Anacons, two Tibbies and one horror of a flying Sool. Oh, my, and they are all armed. They'll be here any minute now, you must all flee!"

"Calm down, Sparkie. We can't leave Migo here, and his leg is caught in the mouth of a snake." Hella took command.

"Look, I want you to penetrate the rock and see what you can do to make it let go."

As she spoke, she scanned the tunnel, looking for a place for us to hide ourselves. We could already hear the heavy footfall of the Tibbies and the rattle of the Sool's bat-like leathery wings. The Broomaks and the Anacons advanced silently and I felt the skin crawl on my back as I waited, hardly daring to breathe.

I had never fought a battle of any kind in my whole life. It was frightening to imagine how we could possibly survive against those strong and armed opponents. I wished I could run away from this dangerous confrontation and never look back. After all, these beings were criminals who would stop at nothing to save their prize. And they were sought by law enforcement groups throughout the known universe for their heinous crime. There was a huge price on their heads. They were desperate and dangerous, and I wanted no part of them.

Then I thought of Princess Liss. She needs my

help, I remembered. I felt that without me, she may never be free again! My heart did a buck and wing as I thought how gratefully affectionate she would feel toward me.

Migo's placid face turned from pale grey to crimson as he tried to wrestle his foot from out of the snake's jaws. There was no time to lose! I wondered what Sparkie was doing down there, since he surely wasn't doing anything to stun the reptile or make it let go. Sheer unadulterated fear had my hands shaking like two leaves as I touched Hella on one shoulder. Having thus gotten her attention, I whispered, "Hella, we'll have no chance if we try to stand up to them here in the open passage; we'll have to hide somewhere."

"By all the blessed Trintors " don't you think I know that?" she exploded. "Why is it that you males just lose it when you are faced with a challenge? When faced with a problem to solve, you all just dissolve in redundancies and whimpers. I really don't understand how you came to be the dominant sex in so many humanoid cultures!" Her eyes shot out little sparks of impatience. "Instead of stating the obvious, why don't you come up with a suggestion? Surely you don't expect me to come up with the perfect hideaway?"

"Wwell…" I stammered uncertainly. "I didn't know I was stating the obvious, but I guess you're right." I tried to think where we could hide ourselves, with or without Migo, as the case might be. The rustling of leathery wings could be heard somewhere just down the corridor. I looked and saw that Migo's face had turned purple as he struggled to free himself in vain.

"Sparkie, hurry, hurry!" he begged. The grip on his ankle only tightened with each movement he made.

My knees buckled under me with fright as a dark, flying projectile shot out from the mysterious darkness of the passage ahead and flew straight at us. In my imagination I could feel the Sool's sharp claws tearing at my flesh. I felt nauseated for a moment and closed my eyes, then swallowed fast several times and opened them again. In that instant Migo gasped and rolled away on the rocky surface behind me, having been finally released from the serpent's deadly embrace. Sparkie had done the job, after all, for in that moment I felt him back in the space above my head, twinkling triumphantly.

The Sool bypassed me altogether and with a terrifying cry, sped past my head and attacked Hella, no doubt attracted by her pugnacious stance. Hella caught the creature in the beam of her stun-gun, leaping sideways at the same time in order to avoid being crushed by the leathery horror as it fell. At this point, I collected my wits and unholstered my own stun-gun, directing its beam at the enemy. From out of the corner of my eye, I saw that Migo did the same from his position on the floor.

Remembering my teachings, I tried to communicate with the enemy, linking minds to establish contact with a view to convincing it we meant no harm, we would not kill or maim, and would rather lay down all arms and negotiate in friendship. I projected thoughts of universal love and peace. Unfortunately, the creature was in a fighting frenzy and beyond my reach.

Silently, stealthily, the Broomaks appeared from the depths of the passage, one by one. I had no time to appraise their appearance because the Anacons weren't far behind. Their hissing was heard mere yards away. Then a Tibbie emerged, a tall, shaggy creature with a wild face and a mouth full of long, sharp teeth. I definitely wanted to steer clear of this one! The creatures were all armed with blasters, stunners, and an assortment of weapons completely foreign to me.

I pushed the button on my Gravi-T-belt and lifted off the floor. It was imperative to find a safe retreat for us all before it was too late. The Sool, seeing me rise, imagining that I was escaping, attacked me. I hit it with a maximum blast from my stun-gun, but the distance was too great; it swayed but didn't react.

Then I got a crazy idea. My belt was equipped with the Sylix rings amplifier, meant to use in collecting samples from far planets and bring them home alive. The Sylix rings would place the specimens in cryo-sleep so that they could be transported, undamaged. It was safe to use. Besides, hadn't I learned earlier that the princess herself was being held prisoner, immobilized by three Sylix rings?

I decided to Sylix the Sool. Airborne once again, I made for a vertical shaft leading who-knew-where. I had no luxury of choice with the vengeful Sool at my back. Obviously, he was determined to get me. A beam from his stun-gun passed within inches of my right ear. Activating the force shield operated through the control panel on my belt, I kept accelerating upward with the Sool close behind.

At the end of that shaft was another cavern. I landed gently and waited for the Sool to catch up. Three heartbeats later a dark, leathery body shot out of the shaft, circled above my head and prepared to sweep down and pin me down. By this time, it knew its energy ray had no effect on my shield. It had planned another tactic, that of simply squashing me to death. How did it know my shield could be crushed with slow pressure?

Okay, David, here it comes! The Sool moved in, claws extended, ready to catch me in a flattening embrace. Don't panic, my boy, just wait until it's close enough before you activate. I fired. The rings of Sylix fell around the Sool and tightened instantaneously as the cooling action began. He went to sleep with such a surprised expression that I couldn't resist a chuckle as the shimmering, light blue force field of the outer ring folded his wings while the inner ring put him in peaceful cryo-sleep.

CHAPTER 17

Pushing my Gravi-T-belt starter again, I hastened back to my friends, feeling certain they would need me in their unevenly-matched battle with the guardians of the stolen treasure.

The passageway below was a terrifying sight to behold. Hella bled from many cuts to her face, head and arms, her protective suit cut to shreds. She was presently engaged in battle with two Broomaks and one Tibbie. Fortunately, Hella was expert in the martial arts skills of ten different star systems, and was using every kick and blow she knew to hold her attackers at bay while Migo, who was puny of limbs, was in deep trouble, as usual. I saw that now it was an Anacon that held Migo in its grip as it tightened its scaly, slimy limbs around him in order to squeeze the very stuffing out of him. Sparkie was above, keeping the other attackers entertained and occupied with all manner of illusions and tricks.

Deciding that Migo needed my help most of all, I landed at his side. The Anacon is a creature with five different brain centers located in each of its long, snakelike necks. In order to save my friend, I would have to paralyze all five of the Anacon's brains.

Uh, oh! Maybe it's too late! Migo's face was distorting with a terrible grimace of asphyxiation. The Anacon was so busy strangling its victim that it ignored me completely. That was a mistake. I rested my stun-gun against one of its heads and fired. The beast shook convulsively and Migo cried out in anguish as fresh blood oozed from his old wounds. I located the second brain and fired again, with the same result. One of the three remaining heads detached itself from the serpent and looked straight at me with slitty, evil eyes and spat at the very same moment I fired and put that brain out of commission, too.

The venomous saliva hit my force field and sizzled like acid. Whoa! I thought. I wouldn't want to smell that one's breath! It looked like the saliva could corrode metal!

With two more brains left, the creature let go of Migo and went after me. Quickly, I calculated the distance between us; it was just right. As the Anacon's tendril reached out for me, I aimed the rings of Sylix and they fell on my surprised enemy before it touched my shield.

Two down. I sighed deeply and looked around. Hella was a clever girl. She noticed how I had used my Sylix device and followed suit, immobilizing one of the slow, bearlike Tibbies and a couple of the Broomaks in short order. Good!

That makes five. The Broomaks were ugly, bony monoliths with no flesh, and their nervous systems and veins located inside their bones, giving them a skeleton-like appearance except for the incongruous growth of hair on their heads. This, indeed, was a life form of spectacular proportion and structure. Unfortunately, I had no time to wonder about the geological and climatical conditions which would foster such a child of nature.

Migo scrambled to his feet and I jumped in beside him. Together, we began to fight back to back. Two remaining Anacons and one Tibbie attacked simultaneously with lasers and other weapons. Migo and I both had the protection of our energy shields, now, but I wasn't at all sure they would hold under the force of the blasts. We did the best we could with our stun-guns, which wasn't much, since, as I mentioned, you have to fire the things at point-blank range for maximum effectiveness.

The Tibbie saw that its ray-gun was having no effect and tried instead to stampede us with its large, hairy body. I activated my Gravi-T-belt and shot up, dragging the hapless Migo with me, just in time. However, one of the Anacons managed to get hold of Migo's ankles and was dragging us downward with all its weight. I pulled up, the Anacon pulled down, and Migo screeched in pain. One of the Tibbies was stretching up its hairy arms to grasp the escaping victim, too. Wonderful!

Encircling Migo' limp body with both hands, I could neither activate his Gravi-T-belt nor access my Sylix device. Why was Migo limp? I shook him once, twice. "Migo! Wake up! Come on, fella, you've chosen a fine time to faint on me!" Despite the downward tugging by the Anacon, I shook Migo as hard as I could until I felt some life returning to him.

"Migo! Activate your Gravi-T, and shoot that serpent with your Sylix, now!" Miraculously, while I held on to him for dear life, he did as I ordered. The massive body of the Anacon slid heavily to the floor as it began to curl up in cryo-sleep.

"Good for you, Migo!" I yelled. "That makes six! Are you okay now, buddy? I'm going to let go!" He nodded and a gurgle of assent escaped from the back of his throat. I let go. He shot up under the boost of his Gravi-T, without me or the Anacon to restrain him, and let out a blood-curdling yell as he hit his head on the passage ceiling.

Poor Migo, he'd gone through so much pain in the space of one short day. Just as he bit his lip in determination to be brave, a remaining Tibbie ignored me and reached for my friend just before I let him have a dose of my Sylix rings.

Despite the fact that Migo weighed well over two hundred pounds, he had passed out again and was gently bumping the roof as he bobbed on his Gravi-T. I knew he was suffering and should be taken to a safe place. I turned my attentions, instead, to the remaining Tibbie. But Hella beat me to it, turning her Sylix device on the creature as it rushed at her, and dropping it in its tracks.

Three Broomaks remained. I left them to Hella and directed my attention to getting Migo down off the ceiling. I turned off his Gravi-T-belt and flew him up the shaft to the cavern where I lay him gently on the floor and wiped the poisonous saliva the first Anacon had left on his leg and foot. Unfortunately, the stuff had eaten through both his suit and his flesh, and the stench was of rotting meat. His wounds had turned an unhealthy shade of blue.

What can I do? I searched my pockets feverishly. Sure enough, I had shoved a spray tube of the Unibac in there from my last doctoring on the ship. I sprayed the stuff liberally on his poisoned flesh and then, on the second thought, opened his mouth and sprayed his throat as a deterrent against infection, in case he'd breathed any of the poison in. He swallowed. Good! That should stop the blood poisoning. I repeated the entire procedure, just in case. His wounds would stay open and draining until we got back to the ship and he was able to heal properly. I left him to sleep it off and flew back to Hella.

The dear girl had managed to immobilize one of the Broomaks and still fought with the remaining two of them in a fierce battle to the death, with Sparkie flitting around desperately, unable to do anything to help. Circling Hella and the Broomaks, I saw that she was very much worse for the wear. She bore several deep gashes on her forearms and bleeding wounds on her head and shoulders. Worse still, her beautiful ruff had been partially torn from her neck and lay peeled back, soaked with blood, the pink inner flesh exposed. They've tried to skin her! I gasped inwardly. I couldn't endure the sight.

Taking aim, I immobilized the first Broomak and then the other with the Sylix rings.

The last remaining Anacon was gliding toward us and preparing for attack, all five heads waving simultaneous in a hypnotic dance of death.

"Sparkie," I called, "can you spook the Anacon or something to distract it while I get Hella out of here?

Our invisible friend flashed an "okay" and created the illusion of ten Hellas and ten Davids, disorienting the slimy creature, who didn't know which to attack first.

Meanwhile, I righted up Hella's real body and activated my Gravi-T, flying rapidly to the cavern, where I propped her against the sleeping Migo. Quickly, I sprayed Hella's wounds and tore a piece off her suit to wrap the hanging fur back against her neck. It wasn't much, but it would have to do.

I flew back to where Sparkie was still entertaining the bewildered Anacon. The thing was charging the air, poison dripping from its fanged mouths, as I stunned two of its heads. In spite of everything, I felt sorry for the beast, which was so clearly outmatched. I think the Anacon knew it too, but it wasn't going to give up without a monumental struggle. It coiled itself into a ball to nurse its injured heads, and I had the feeling it would spring into action again any minute.

Then I had an idea. I wasn't at all sure if it would work, but it was worth a try while the beast was still disoriented. The idea was simple. It was the love projection we often practiced at the Academy. I closed my eyes and went into a light trance from which I projected feelings of peace and love. I could see the Anacon with my third eye and it was regarding me suspiciously. I continued to send out images of peace and love. Then I accompanied the images with a message to cease all antagonism toward us and no harm would come to it as a result.

"Anacon, deep in your minds you must know you're on the wrong track; know you are wrong, know how mistaken you are to pursue an aggressive course of action." I could see with my third eye that the creature was considering. I continued my projection with more insistence. I told it to look deep inside its mind for the answer; asked it to be my friend; as a friend, told it not to attack. No response came from the creature. It stared straight at me unwaveringly, yet I had the distinct sensation it was softening. I hoped so. If it had sprung at me while I was meditating, I would have been mincemeat! But I was too far into this experiment to turn back. Insane or not, I had to make an attempt at dominating this beast.

I let myself regain a wide-awake state and spoke aloud for the first time.

"Anacon, I am going to approach you now. I will leave my weapons here on the floor to show you that I will not harm you."

What if this backfires? I inwardly cringed at the thought. After all, it's one thing to preach on the universality of goodness and love back at the Academy, but how do they know it for an empirical fact?

I took a step, then another and another. The beast didn't move. We looked into each other's eyes for a few nerve-racking moments, then I stretched my hands out, palm up, in a friendly manner and advanced again. The Anacon stared at my hands with three working eyes and then closed them all and lowered his heads to the ground in submission.

Tears of relief and joy rolled down my freckled cheeks. I wanted to embrace the slimy thing and congratulate it on its victory over evil, but the remembrance of that acid saliva caused me to restrain myself at the last minute. My heart was full of pride for the battle we had won over the forces of destruction, and I knew I would never again doubt anything the Academy had taught me.

CHAPTER 18

When my friends awakened, somewhat refreshed although by no means healed from their ordeals, I explained our current status and asked if they felt up to helping me. Then we worked together to round up all the combatants, move them into the cavern and secure them together with an outer band of Sylix rings. All save my subdued Anacon, that is. I couldn't help thinking of it as "my" Anacon, although contact between us was sketchy at best. Nevertheless, this exceptional serpentine creature had clearly thrown his cooperation in with our mission, although it was not easy to convince my friends of this.

We remained in the cavern long enough to eat-a brief meal and take an even briefer rest. Needless to say, we were exhausted. Sparkie stood watch while we slept and we awoke more refreshed to tend to each other's wounds and prepare to march toward our destinies. Oh, what we wouldn't have given for a sonic shower at the time!

My new friend's name was Tsuin, or at least that's how I spelled the approximation of the sound of it. Tsuin warned us that the triple ring of sylix which imprisoned the Princess was controlled and operated by the Loxie stones. He, himself, had no knowledge of how to unlock the code. I felt the responsibility was going to fall on me, and after the last zapping I took in punishment for my meddling with the boulder-door, I did not relish my next mental link with the stones. What if I died with the next zap? Then the image of the Princess came back into my mind and I knew I was ready to die, if need be, if that's what it took to save her.

Half an hour later we reached the room with the table upon which the Loxie stones rested in their glowing cubicles. The room looked exactly as it had in my trance, and was dark except for the illumination from the stones. A few feet further along a corridor and we located the room holding the Princess. Locked inside a Sylix cell was the girl of my dreams, along with many treasures stolen from other star systems and undoubtedly listed as missing in intergalactic police files. This was a lucky find, indeed! Whether we ended this adventure alive or dead, we were already heroes of the first magnitude on the strength of this discovery alone, of that I was sure.

We could see many cases of nal, the most precious metal in the universe, and trays of brilliant crimson gallix stones, the smallest of which would cost me a whole year's food tokens. More open cases glinted dimly in the available light from our belt torches and we could see gold and platinum and rare nal coins from a thousand different star systems.

Then we gasped, as we spotted the most prized booty of all, those silver cases emblazoned with a pharmaceutical star that could only mean they contained a cache of omnivac, the miracle vaccine capable of eradicating all the disease in the universe. It had been stolen in a daring scheme pulled off by unknown thieves in the Omnivac Laboratories in Plaedoon fifty standard years ago. Tragically, the thieves had accidentally frightened to death the old scientific genius, Dr. Olaf Omni, in his lab at the time of the break-in. Dr. Omni had the formula committed to memory, having trusted it to no one in the universe except himself, and when he died of cardiac arrest, the formula died with him, without even a sample of the precious vaccine remaining which could be analyzed for duplication by his colleagues.

I realized I had stopped breathing while I contemplated the magnitude of this discovery and I gasped in an attempt to fill my lungs before turning to my companions. "Do you know what this means? We can give the Omnivac back to the universe. A way will be found to reproduce it when they have the model, and Dr. Omni's life work will serve all living things as it was meant to do. Gosh, guys, I'm so excited I can hardly stand it!"

"You must be," smiled Hella, "you've forgotten all about your dream girl and here she is right under your nose!"

"Oh, right." I was embarrassed now. "Listen, I'll leave you to figure out how to inventory this stuff and get it back to the ship while I go to work on those stones."

It took me a long time to tune in to their complicated vibrations, especially since I had to be careful not to provoke a sudden discharge of energy from them like last time. Finally locating the stone which was keyed to the lock on the cell of the princess, I requested its release. One thing at a time. At least this request wasn't met by a blinding, searing flash of light in my cerebral cortex. The confirmation which came was telepathic, and I thanked the stone for its cooperation before breaking rapport and opening my eyes to seek out my friends.

CHAPTER 19

The door to the princess' cell was standing open and my friends were already inside, moving the heavy boxes out with the aid of their Gravi-T-belt propulsion. I walked inside and stood for countless minutes, transfixed at what I beheld. Without my asking the Loxie stones, the rings of Sylix were dissolving and the color of roses was returning to Princess Liss o'Diss's cheeks. She was more enchanting than I ever imagined. Pale, fair-haired and delicate, she had a little glow emanating from her body like an aura of moonlight.

The princess lay unmoving on a marbled stone bench, clad only in a milky translucent robe, the same one in which she had been reported kidnapped from her sleeping chambers, and she looked fragile and sweet. I guessed she wasn't tall, but her youth and slenderness of form lent her a fairy-like ethereal appearance that mesmerized me.

Then she shuddered and moaned softly before opening her eyes and blinking at me.

I started to speak, but the words never got past the lump in my throat. What do you say to the most exquisite Princess in the universe?

"Who are you?" She spoke in a weak but imperious voice.

"And where am I?"

I cleared my throat a couple of times and tried to think where to begin to tell her about all this. She must have been put to sleep with the rings of Sylix at the moment of her kidnapping.

"Are you mute? Don't you know I could have your eyes put out for daring to ogle me in this manner! Speak, if you will. I wish to know where I am, who you are and what is going on!" Her voice was stronger now, and she was clearly angry.

"I ... I am called David, Your Highness. I am one of a special team who came to rescue you from this prison."

"Prison? Where? How?"

"I'm afraid this is going to be a shock for you, Your Highness, but you were kidnapped a very long time ago in a scandal that rocked the universe. You have been preserved by the rings of Sylix in cryo-sleep ever since. On this day we succeeded in defeating your captors and throwing rings of Sylix over them so that they can be returned to stand trial before the Galactic Council for their misdeeds."

She stared at me for what seemed an eternity. Slowly, recognition came into her eyes, then belief, as she remembered that moment back in her chambers before the rings were thrown. Her expression softened and she smiled. I melted, I wanted to compose a sonata to her smile and build a monument to her incredible eyes. I have never seen such eyes and I am a guy who is very partial to beautiful eyes!

"Could you support me while I try to get up?" She widened those eyes at me. "I really must have been Sylixed for a long time; I have no strength in my muscles. What I really need is an hour on an Ergociser to tone me up again."

In my haste to comply with a humane request, I neglected to be intimidated by her exalted presence and before you could say happily ever after I had my arm around her, supporting her, propping her up while she bowed her head and moved her fingers against her temples in concentric circles.

"Just take it easy, Your Highness. You'll probably be somewhat dizzy for the first little while. I'll walk you outside, and find a safe place to wait while Migo brings the ship up to this terrace, just as soon as you're feeling up to it. "

"Where are we …? What did you say you are called?"

"David, Your Highness. We are on the Planet Dido in the Syph nebulae. More precisely, we are in the heart of a mountain which is reached through a labyrinth of tunnels. We have marked them with luminous arrows to facilitate our exit."

"How many are in your party, David? Are you bounty hunters, or police, or what?"

"We are an expedition of four, Your Highness, from the Academy on Teenpon, assigned to rescue Your Highness from captivity and to deliver the treasure to the Galactic council as well as take into custody the perpetrators who must be returned to stand trial."

"And are your companions all as young as you,

David? Why, you're still just a boy! I wonder that you would be given such a perilous assignment at such a tender age. You have been very brave."

"I'm not that tender, Your Highness. I've already turned eighteen. And, if I may say so, Your Highness, you don't look a day older, yourself!"

She laughed, and it was the sound of crystal bells in the breeze. "You have made your point, my friend. I do tend to get carried away with myself at times. Blame it on my royal upbringing." She pointed one dainty toe and circled an ankle to hasten the return of circulation. "Now, who did you say your team is composed of, and where did you say they are?"

It was my turn to chuckle. "I didn't, Your Highness, but since you ask, I will. May I?" I knelt down and took first one little foot, then the other, between my hands and rubbed them until they glowed pink and warm. And as I rubbed, I explained, "My friends are Hella, Migo and Sparkie. Hella is from O'Bria. Migo is a Gorgon. Sparkie is a pure-energy being, and I'm a Terran from the Milky Way Galaxy. We're all graduating students of the Teenpon Academy and, as I said before, this was the seventh of the twelve Herculean Tasks we must perform in order to become diplomats."

"Oh, I think I understand. Thank you for rubbing my feet. Could you help me to stand now?" She offered an elegant hand.

"Up and around already? That was fast work, David. You did good. Greetings, Princess, and welcome to the Quintux Century!" Hella stood in the entrance to the cell, all slinky, saucy and flaming furry seven feet of her, hands on hips and golden eyes flashing approvingly.

"This is Hella, Your Highness." At this, Hella swiftly strode to where the Princess stood, somewhat uncertainly, and nearly crushed her in an unceremonious embrace.

"Yes," came a smothered reply. "I see. I'm glad to meet you, Hella, and I am in your debt for saving me. In debt to all of you," she added, for clarity.

Minutes later, Princess Liss o'Diss repeated the haphazard formality of introduction and greetings with my other two friends, neither of whom had ever been educated in court procedure any more than Hella and I had. Only Migo managed to pull himself together into something resembling courtly behavior when he rather clumsily kissed her hand and cut his lip on her faceted gallix stone ring.

When Her Royal Highness was strong enough to walk the maze of tunnels leading to the outer world, she could not avoid meeting up with the Tsuin and nearly fainted from fright, although I took care to explain in advance. How could we blame her for being horrified at the proximity of such a revolting creature, in a conscious state, on the same ship? But she was a pragmatist by nature and soon reconciled herself to the practical aspect of Tsuin's alliance.

Meanwhile, I made her as comfortable as possible in the master cabin aboard the ship, and showed her how to play the Telescan and use the ship's reference library to catch up on all that had happened historically while she had slept in the rings of Sylix.

Once I had the princess safe and sound aboard our craft, I returned to assist my friends in the transportation of the Sylixed guards we had left in the chamber. Using our Gravi-T-belts for propulsion, we half pushed, half flew them out to the ship one by one, with three of us pushing, tugging and balancing while Sparkie gave directions and led the way.

It was a good thing the princess had lots and lots of intergalactic newscasts and history to catch up on, because the evacuation of prisoners took all that day and the better part of two additional planetary revolutions before we got the perpetrators stowed away.

On the fourth day after I had broken the Princess' bonds of Sylix -- funny how I was dating everything from that occurrence as if time had been born in that instant – we began carting all the treasure to the ship. It took us nearly a week to relocate it all. All except for the Loxie stones, that is. No one mentioned the stones; it was as if we were all avoiding the inevitable. Moving the stones implied an obvious danger and serious preparations were needed, so we left it to the last.

Finally, we met to brainstorm the challenge of moving the stones. They had been placed in their resting place in the mountain many years ago and throughout the years had made contract with some of the crystalline mineral which the mountain contained, developed a strong rapport -- the kind required to control movement of boulders like that which had blocked our tunnel earlier. No matter how long and hard I had tried to influence the stones, through meditation, I couldn't persuade them to break rapport with the mountain which held them captive.

I needed an inspiration. When everyone was gathered in the ship's lounge, I presented the challenge.

"It is entirely possible that the Loxie stones have affected lower life forms on this planet, life forms which will also come to their aid if we try to forcibly remove them from this habitat," observed Migo. Hella quickly interjected, "I noted the phosphorescent moss back in those tunnels and suspect it has a mind of its own. And, because it's elementary cellular structure precludes the possibility of its having intelligence as we define it, one can only guess it is influenced by the stones."

"Don't forget those bloodthirsty birds out there," shimmered Sparkie.

It was Migo's turn again. "If the stones can influence all living matter on this planet, what might they cause us to do?" He shivered at the thought.

Princess Liss held up a hand to indicate a wish for our attention. "I can add that the Loxie stones hold very fast to friendships. Once they link up, it's impossible to break the bond without incurring some form of disaster," she said thoughtfully. When the bandits wrested the stones from Laoria, there were major quakes and fires that lay the capital in ruin and destroyed half the planet. Countless thousands of citizens died. We must heed that example and take extreme precautions."

"This is really serious, then," said Hella. "All we've been through is beginning to seem like the entre and now we're going for the main course!"

"You know better than to talk food at me when I'm nervous or worried," pleaded Migo. "Now I'm in the mood for something sweet."

"Sorry, forget I said it," rejoined Hella. "We've pledged to keep you on your diet. I'll look for better analogies in future."

"Well, anyway," pouted Migo. "We can't leave the Stones behind because it's part of our Task to return with them. What are we to do?"

"There is no safe way," Princess Liss o'Diss spoke in a voice of command. "We must grab the Stones and run for the ship, and hope to lift off our terrace before the planet twists itself into a corkscrew with its grief over the parting."

We knew what this implied. A hush fell over our group. We accepted this solution as the only possible course of action, given the elements we knew to be operative in the situation.

"Tomorrow, then." I straightened up, unaware until that instant that I had been hunched forward, my body tense and strained. Everyone nodded. Tomorrow we would make the transfer. Tomorrow we might all die. We bid each other good night. Tomorrow will come soon enough.

CHAPTER 20

After performing our morning duties the next day, we all gathered in the chamber where the stones lay. Today they were glowing with a specially bright luminescence, as if they knew about our plan and were prepared to do battle with us. The plan was to wrap each stone in an insulating material which would baffle the strength of their emissions. Each of us carried a drawstring purse hung on our belts wherein we would carry as many stones as would fit, and between the four of us we would carry them all. This time Princess Liss was the fourth member of our party, and Sparkie stayed behind with the ship.

We were ready. Looking around at the other pale faces, I knew mine must look the same. Scared to death! The Princess nodded the signal to begin and without a sound we began lifting, wrapping and stowing the Stones in our bags. We worked with all the speed we could muster while we tried to ignore the strange tingling sensations we received from the touch of a Stone upon the flesh of our hands.

We heard a rumbling from deep within the mountain. Dido wanted to keep her treasures, as we suspected. As we wrapped the stones, the rumbling grew stronger and a few rocks rattled past outside, down the tunnel-way. The mountain was stirring, getting ready to strike back. And I didn't like the sounds it was making, didn't like it at all.

Just a few more Stones to go. I, who almost never perspired unless the weather was intolerably muggy, was profusely sweating now. I was shivering, too, and my teeth were chattering. It was fear; I feared something would happen to trap us in the mountain forever. Then the job was done and all the Stones were secured. Migo gave us the signal to retreat and we activated our Gravi-T-belts for propulsion as soon as we were outside in the tunnel. As we were leaving the chamber, a wall collapsed with a thunderous noise and I was glad Hella, Migo and the Princess had gotten out of there ahead of me.

Down the tunnels we flew, guided by our phosphorescent markings of old. A jagged piece of rock fell from a rift in the rock wall above out heads and caught the Princess on one cheek, giving her a nasty cut. I saw the blood gush from the wound and my heart wrenched for her pain. But there was no time to stop and medicate her, for we had another half a mile of tunnels to go before we reached the entrance to the cave.

Onward we raced, and I hoped the rock walls surrounding us will not collapse and bury us all right here. We would never be found. A roar went through the mountain as I finished my thought and big cracks appeared in the passage before us. From far below, I could smell sulfur seeping up from the volcanic core and wondered how long it would take before the inevitable explosion. There was no stopping now, despite the fact that Migo had been hit by another falling rock, had passed out, and was being towed by Hella.

I looked over at the Princess. She was still bleeding all over her robe look. She was looking very drained and weak, but she kept up with the rest of us as we accelerated along tunnels which were beginning to break up and crumble, the Loxie Stones bouncing innocently on our hips. As we flew, I tried desperately to make contact with the force that was causing the breakup of this mountain, but all I came in contact with was a vortex of fury somewhere deep in its bowels, and there was no way to develop a rapport with that.

Readjusting the bag of stones on my hip, I calmed the wild beating of my heart and noticed there was more light in the tunnel now. We were close to the entrance cave.

"We made it!" shouted Hella, who leaped into the bottom of the cave and lowered Migo to the floor.

Then the whole mountain shook like a toy that had been picked up and rattled by some giant hand, and the cave crumpled around us just as I followed the Princess out of the tunnel. Instinctively, I reached for her to shelter her body with mine and saw a shower of stars behind my eye lids as we went down under a pile of stone rubble.

I don't know how long we stayed there. When I

came around, the place looked unreal. My mind was sluggish and I couldn't remember what I was doing in this place. Then the memories returned and I tried in vain to move. What? Buried alive? My worst fear is realized! My mind shrank from the prospect of this slow and horrible death. Every bone in my body felt broken; there wasn't a single nerve that didn't feel the pain, yet I sensed that I was not seriously injured.

Then I realized I was lying across on top of Princess Liss. How ironic that a tremor would be a vehicle to get us together in a physical way. She moaned and I quickly asked, "Princess! Your Highness, are you all right?"

"I'm not sure," came her shaky reply, in a voice that was weak and trembling. "Can you move off me?"

"No. I'm sorry, but the plain truth of the matter is we're buried under a jumble of rocks."

"Oh. How are we going to get free?" she inquired in a small but composed voice.

"I don't know. I can't lie to you. It looks pretty bad. Yet, if Hella or Migo survived the rock fall, they may be able to dig us out."

Princess Liss sighed. Then a new thought occurred to me. "Wait," I said. "I forgot Sparkie is still aboard the ship. If we don't return in good time, I'm sure he'll come out to scout us. Then he'll think of something to do," I said reassuringly.

"Oh, Dave, you are so bright," she whispered. I was glad she couldn't see the confusion on my face, let alone the blush. I didn't know what to say and felt at a loss. As if guessing what an emotional turmoil her words had thrown me into, she shifted slightly and pressed her cheek to my hand. My chest almost burst open with joy.

She likes me! She does! My mind sang, and for a moment I forgot our desperate situation, forgot about everything but my Princess as time froze for a moment and became solid like a crystal drop.

"Do you think there's a way the Loxie Stones can help us out of this dilemma?" she asked, startling me out of my reverie.

"Well, I don't know. Perhaps if we both try to communicate together, we can generate enough mental energy for contact. But we must clearly project our location and that of the ship, so that if the stones move this rubble, they move the appropriate sections of it."

"Yes. Good idea," she replied. "By the way, have you noticed how lightly this rubble is piled over us, pinning us down but not crushing us under its weight?"

"Yes, now that you mention it," I agreed. The mass of rubble, although conforming to our fallen positions, was about an inch away from our bodies.

"I don't recall activating my shield. Did you?"

"No. Could the stones have activated our shields, do you think? Could they be feeling protective of us?"

"I don't know. Maybe. Now, Princess, if Your Highness will excuse me, I must enter a light mediational trance in order to scout the cave and locate my friends."

She fell silent and I closed my eyes.

First of all, I looked for Hella and Migo. There

they were, only a few feet away, pressed to the ground by a huge boulder that pinned them without crushing in the same curious manner as the rubble imprisoning the Princess and me. Hella was unconscious, just like Migo, but both were alive. Now Migo was coming around. I projected telepathically.

"Migo! This is Dave. We are all pinned by the cave-in, but I think I can get us out, soon. Hang in there, buddy!"

In my mind's eye, I saw that Sparkie had piloted our ship to the terrace outside the cave, where it hovered expectantly. I reached out to him telepathically.

"Sparkie! Calm yourself. We're all alive and pinned in the entrance to the cave under a rock rubble. I'm going to try communicating with the stones to see if they'll correct this situation, but if that fails, I'll get back to you, so we can think of some other way to drill or blast our way out. Meanwhile, keep the ship clear of the mountain if you register an eruption coming, okay?"

I knew I could trust Sparkie to carry out my instruction to the letter. Returning to the conscious realm, I explained my actions to Princess Liss, who remained relatively calm and indicated she was ready to link minds with me. We counted down, and with two minds linked as one, made contact with the Loxie stones. Clearly, they were distressed and at first resisted contact. We persisted, and at last they grew quiet as if listening.

"Oh, esteemed Loxie stones, heart and soul of O'Venti, in your wisdom, hear our plea. You must stop this disaster. Do not allow the destruction of this beautiful planet on which many creatures depend for live support. Your struggle is pointless as you do not belong here on Dido. Your true home is on Laoria and our mission is to see that you are returned there. So we ask that you cooperate and cease this violence before it is too late." The Stones shimmered.

Good! We had them thinking about the issue at hand.

"Oh wise Stones of O'Venti', we ask but one more thing. We require your assistance in clearing our path to the ship, so that we may board with you and begin your journey home. You are in rapport with the energy of this mountain, and we ask that you use that rapport to free us from our rocky grave."

We opened our eyes and waited. One minute dragged by, two minutes, and nothing. "Let's try again," I said. We closed our eyes and resumed contact. I repeated the message over and over again. Then somewhere deep in the heart of the mountain we felt a stirring and then a stillness broken only by the occasional gurgle of steam still escaping through the fissures in the rock. Evidently the Stones had decided to believe me.

Then a miracle occurred. The rubble above us shifted and began rolling off to pile itself harmlessly at the side of the cave. Soon, I was able to roll off the Princess and sit up. She scrambled to her knees and then reached over to hug me.

"We did it!" she cried happily. The blood had dried on her face and gown, and she was all dusty and tousled, but she looked like an angel. Together we crawled over to Hella and Migo. Hella was just coming around. She complained of a severe headache, but otherwise seemed okay. Migo was pulling himself together and dusting off. We all looked for the entrance to the cave and, squinting through the haze, I saw that the stone rubble had shifted just enough for us to walk through.

"Let's go," I said and led the way for a few steps when I realized the haze hadn't lifted. I rubbed my eyes and asked Migo, "Does it seem hazy in here to you?"

"Not at all," he said. "You might try wearing your glasses, though."

My glasses? I felt my face. He was right; they were not there. I looked around, then doubled back briefly to cast a look around for them. Everything was fuzzy. Ha! I thought. I need to wear my glasses in order to find my glasses!

The others were outside the cave now, and I had to decide whether to call one of them back to help me look, or join them. I decided to cut my losses and get out of there before the mountain changed its mind about blowing a fuse. It felt odd, losing the final remnant of my Terran identity like that. Now I would be obliged to have that laser surgery everyone at the Academy insisted would instantly cure my myopia with no pain and no down time for recuperation. For the time being, however, my vision was extremely limited and I had to watch my every step except with things I could focus on at close range.

We boarded the ship and just as it lifted off the

terraced shelf that whole section of the canyon collapsed into itself. It was terrifying to watch on the screen, and I was thankful not to be a part of it. By mutual agreement, we decided not to stick around and monitor the damage. Quickly Migo accelerated the ship to the outer envelope of the planet and from there we made our jump into hyperspace.

Chapter 21

Once underway, we set to the task of inventorying the considerable treasure and worked around the clock until it was all tabulated in the computer. Liss was at my side during most of the time, as open-mouthed in admiration of this fantastic wealth as we were. Ironically enough, while she's slept for decades in the same room with this booty, she never knew it was there.

My thoughts would always become confused with Liss nearby, especially now that she had asked me to drop my use of the formal title of "Princess" and just use her first name. I suspected she said this in order to make us all more comfortable and relaxed with her on our long journey back to Teenpon, yet a small part of myself interpreted it as an intimate privilege which might have a deeper meaning to me.

Does she like me in a special way, or is she just showing friendly gratitude to a guy who will soon be a folk hero? I wondered. Every so, often I would catch her watching me with a tender little smile on her lips and I wondered what to make of it.

While we were cataloging the collection of priceless art objects stolen from Aldenoor, I marveled over the exquisite musical instruments which looked like giant crystal wind chimes. I knew they were played by skilled musicians who blew at them through a special amplification device that produced the most heavenly melodies. Liss was captivated by some holo-paintings of unsurpassed beauty, and together we inspected the cases upon cases of unique jewelry set with rare stones.

"Can you recognize any of these treasures as originating on your home world?" Liss asked me smilingly.

"Oh, no! Terra is not that evolved. It is one of the restricted planets, you see," I explained.

"You come from a restricted world?" She looked as if she plainly didn't believe me. Her beautiful eyes were wide with amazement.

"How interesting!" She tried to mask her curiosity. "I've never met anyone before who came from a restricted world. You must tell me all about Terra. For instance, is its restricted status permanent or temporary?"

"Temporary, but that could mean many centuries of Terran time, you know," I replied. "It really all depends on how long it takes the inhabitants to evolve metaphysically."

"Oh, I hope it won't take too long!" she said warmly.

"And since they are all cosmically seeded with the same potential from which you have evolved, it must be ready to bloom in them too. You may not have too long to wait, my friend." She grasped my hand in hers for reassurance and my heart nearly burst out of my chest. I forgot all about Terra or any other place in the universe now that my dream girl was holding my hand, and I wished this moment would never end. I had never been so happy in my young life, and it took a major effort of self-control not to levitate with joy.

CHAPTER 22

Our first destination was Teenpon, where we were received like folk heroes after a radio transmission to the Galactic Council, which related the success of our mission.

When all the fervor of our homecoming died down, arrangements were made by the Council to receive the treasures and restore them to their rightful owners. Meanwhile, the prisoners were brought to trial and sentenced to general reprogramming following a ten-year sentence in the penal colony on Forbidden Planet. Tsuin was the exception; because of his rehabilitated attitude and friendly demeanor he was awarded with immediate reprogramming and given a special appointment as guardian to the Governor's gates.

Are you interested in what happened to the other protagonists in this story? The mastermind behind the kidnapping was Prince Arcobatt Kirin, as had been suspected.

The prince was taken into custody by the IUP (Inter Universe Police) and sentenced to reorientation. In this procedure, a being is divested of titles and possessions, then given brain surgical procedure which repositions the neurons and alters his personality permanently. Following that are years of institutionalization with rehabilitative training and psycho-social reorientation before the individual may return to live as a free citizen once again.

I have obviously avoided the most painful memory of this entire finale, that of the departure of my beloved Princess Liss. Naturally, she returned to her home planet; carrying the Loxie stones and other stolen treasures, but not before she'd been through a long and arduous pre- and post-trial period on Teenpon, not to mention the trials themselves which were a labor for us all, considering the amount of testimony we had to repeat each time a new prisoner came before the court. And not before we collected our reward money and spent part of it on a long vacation on the Pleasure Planet together, where we explored romance and lust and all those raging hormonal expressions so typical of our late-teen psyches.

Hella, Migo and Sparkie vacationed too, and were understanding and patient about keeping their distance when they realized how smitten Liss and I were with each other.

I still hate to relive the moment of her departure in my memory. It still hurts and leaves me with a feeling of emotional desolation. We held hands to the last. We both had tears in our eyes -- I'd had my vision repaired surgically earlier in this anno-quadrant and now I looked fairly acceptable as long as I kept my freckles out of the sun.

"You are a great guy, David," she whispered, "and you're going to be a great man one day. I'll always remember you and hold you dear in my heart. Perhaps you'll come to visit me in the Kingdom of Laoria on O'Venti, when you have completed all twelve of your Herculean Tasks. Will you come?"

"Yes, yes!" I cried. "Oh, precious girl, this must not be the last I'll see of you. I'll only love you more as time goes by."

"Then take me with you in your thoughts and keep safe and well until we meet again." She rose on her toes to kiss my cheek and, before my arms could go around her, she pivoted and left.

I wanted to run after her as she walked up the ramp of the interstellar ship. I wanted to shout her name, tell her I would never love another, that I forbade her to leave me, ever. But I stood there stoically until the ship was airborne.

Later, I thought I caught a glimpse of her winsome face in The Pit, as I was waiting to meet my friends for a drink. In the days to come I thought I saw her everywhere, in the fold of a page, in the petals of a flower, in the fluffy clouds that floated by. I thought of her morning, noon and night, and prayed that we would meet again someday. But I put all this behind me when they called us to receive the assignment number eight.

CHAPTER 23

After a prolonged vacation on Snauru, the pleasure planet, we were assigned to another mission. Since there was nothing more urgent reported in the galaxy at this time, we were sent to Ac'ta system, to prepare the whole system for settlement by pioneers. We were to be the first life-bringers to the barren system.

We brought with us millions of carefully selected seeds to be planted on the planets of the system. Several thousand species of the animal kingdom were to be accommodated there.

That was truly a Herculean Task. It took us five standard years to take care of everything. The moment the first pioneers arrived from all over the galaxy, we were free again.

During those five years, I was in very close contact with Princess Liss. In spite of thousands of light years separating us, we could achieve a telepathic contact instantaneously; we often shared our thoughts and feelings. I missed her terribly, but I still had my tests to pass.

The next one was a real drag. The reports of the

man-eating Dagoo plants on Sigma of the Viminal system were getting more urgent and alarming. When we got there, we had to treat plant after plant with special ultrasonic devices until the last of the plants on the whole system were transformed; the aggressive, man-eating instincts eliminated from their genes forever.

Can you imagine the boredom of such an assignment? Well, at least after this one, I was to meet Princess Liss. She was coming to Teenpon for a few days to attend the Intergalactic Conference of Peace, representing O'Venti, her system. I couldn't wait to meet her.

When the day finally came, I was so excited that it took me an hour of prana-otani breathing exercises to compose myself for the meeting. When I saw her, however, this precious face I had seen in my dreams for years, I forgot about everything, the protocol and all, and hugged her in front of thousands of people unceremoniously. She didn't mind; she threw her arms around my shoulders and kissed me. I was a little upset with myself for blushing. Anyway, during those few happy days on Teenpon, we confessed that we loved each other. I was the happiest man in the universe.

I didn't want to think about the future though. After all, she was a royal princess, and I ... Who was I ...? A nobody from a restricted world. What could I offer her?

But I still had three more tasks to accomplish before I became a fully licensed and respected citizen of the galaxy. For now, the assurance that I loved her and she loved me was enough.

When she embarked on her voyage home, my friends and I went to the committee to get our tenth assignment. The planet Boog in the Essar system needed our help desperately. The accumulation of ice on the polar caps caused the shift of the planet on its axis, causing terrible disasters on the surface. The old mountain chains sunk under the surface of the ocean; the new mountains had erupted on the plains. The flood covered the whole surface of the planet for several standard years. Most of the citizens of Boog died in that cataclysm, but there were still survivors who needed our help.

We were transferred to Boog with instructions to follow emergency procedures. What we found there was pitiful. Nothing remained of the advanced civilization of that planet. The survivors were scattered on boats and rafts, all around the globe and on some of the mountain peaks emerging from the waters. I remembered that something similar had happened on Earth long ago, except that we didn't get help.

Anyway, we did what we could. We built a dozen big floating, unsinkable islands and gathered the survivors on them. Those who were willing to leave the planet, we would transfer to the sister planet of Diox. Those who wanted to remain and wait for the waters to retreat, we equipped with everything they needed for survival until then.

With the job well done, we returned to Teenpon. We didn't have a chance for a break because our next assignment was already chosen for us. There were more and more disturbing reports about Deyan hunters coming to the Committee from the system

Nossiang. There were complaints about the hunters' inhuman practices and cruelty. The blood of the innocent Deyans had been spilled profusely. Their blood had a very special quality; after refining it, it was a powerful, priceless drug, healing all illnesses, physical and mental, and also prolonging life.

Dealing in Sume -- as the drug was called -- was illegal, but many of the great houses and the richest people in the galaxy would offer any price for a vial of the elixir. The sad thing about it was that Deyans were peaceful and intelligent beings. We had orders and permission to apply any drastic measure necessary to end this pointless slaughter, to capture the hunters and bring them to justice. This time we had a convoy of police forces to aid us; seven starships against the intergalactic crime organization. It didn't sound like much, but it would have to do.

When we emerged from light speed near Nossiang, we were immediately attacked by the enemy fighters. We jumped quickly back into hyperspace, where their missiles couldn't reach us. We met with Vasar, the captain of the police forces, to decide what to do. After long debate, we settled for an alternative plan. Migo, Hella, Sparkie and I were to sneak into the system disguised as Sume smugglers or merchants, on a small cargo ship. That way we hoped we could get to the important contacts in the underground organization. It took us some work to camouflage the real features of our ship and transform it into a smuggler's freighter.

We briefed ourselves in our new roles. As soon as we felt comfortable with our new names and characters, we moved on, headed for the main planet of the system Zolla. We cleared our ship as a merchant vessel from Pi Os XI and landed in the overcrowded starport of Fortuna, the capital of Zolla. We disembarked and went for a reconnaissance in the city. It seemed like the most dangerous place I had ever seen, full of vice and crime. The reports said that the gangs of hunters were operating from here. It seemed very possible.

How long could it take to eliminate all this scum? I thought, troubled. I was overwhelmed by the malice I could sense from every corner. The negative vibrations made me feel sick and uneasy. I started to sneeze. Was I allergic to negativity?

I was walking between Migo and Hella, with Sparkie well hidden, squeezed in the pocket of my white coveralls. It wouldn't be wise to walk here with a pure energy being hovering over your head. It could awaken suspicion.

The wide dockside street was crowded and noisy. Street merchants were promoting their products loudly, and brightly painted females from several dozen star systems were looking into our eyes seductively. They smiled at us and waved toward the curtained doors, inviting us to have some fun in exchange for a few credits. An illusion master was entertaining the crowd, conjuring the most fantastic visions in front of the amazed rabble.

The crowd gasped and the credits rolled into the tin box on the ground.

We moved on. A bunch of noisy, drunk Sylvans was kicked out of a bar. The bouncer was a Tibbie. You don't argue with those. We went into the bar. It was called "Under the Brightest Sun", but the interior denied the name. It was dark, gloomy, and it smelled of smaar and the stinking smoke of something I couldn't identify.

We sat behind the bar on tall stools and ordered drinks. The bartender -- an anacon was looking at us suspiciously with his four eyes, while his remaining three heads were deeply engaged in the socatt game across the bar.

We sipped on our drinks quietly and watched and listened. We had to make contact; we had to get into the network of dealers and smugglers, and from there, get to the top of the organization. When the bosses had been dealt with, getting into the hunters' network and eliminating them would be easy. As soon as they lost their leaders, there would be confusion in their ranks and then we could pick them off one by one. It was a hell of a job for us. If our true identities were discovered, we would be exterminated immediately.

I felt nervous. You can't blame me for that.

Suddenly, I felt a heavy hand on my shoulder, and a foul breath hit my nostrils. "Hey, Pal, how you doin'? I have some really good stuff here. Only a thousand credits. What do you say?"

A tall, hairy creature with bloodshot yellow eyes leaned over me. He produced a small vial from the folds of his belt and showed it to me under the bar. The creature might have been an Eryn, but I wasn't sure. Anyway, it stank. Besides, I had my game to play.

"Is it really as good as you say?" asked Hella, coming to my rescue.

"The best. You won't find better Sume in all Fortuna, in all Zolla." The pusher was getting excited.

"We would want to test it," said Migo thoughtfully. "if it is as good as you say, we might be interested in a bigger shipment, like a few gallons, for instance."

"A few gallons?" The Eryn's eyes almost popped out in surprise. "That will cost you a fortune. You could buy an entire planet for that, you know."

"Yes, we know," answered Hella casually. "We are prepared for that expense."

"If you give us a connection with the right people ... people we could make this kind of transaction with ... you'll get your share," Migo lured him. "Let's say a hundred thousand credits. How does that grab you?"

The Eryn's wide lower lip trembled nervously. He also developed a tick in his left eye. "I ... I ... I have to ask around," he stammered.

I felt a little sorry for this creature. He was but a small pawn in the game.

"Okay, we will meet you here tomorrow. Same time. Make sure you contact the right people," said Hella. "We have no time to waste."

We got up and left the bar. "I have a feeling that it might work," I whispered to Migo when we were on the streets. We walked around the city for another few hours, stopping here and there, looking around, making contacts, gathering information.

Finally, tired, we checked into the hotel. It was high time. The night was falling, and on Zolla the nights had to be spent indoors. The temperature soon dropped far below zero, and the winds raging outside could knock an unwary traveler down easily.

I went to the room which I shared with Migo and tried to sleep. I couldn't sleep well; I was too nervous. I dreamed that Princess Liss had been caught by the Deyan hunters and was about to be processed into sume. My own scream awakened me, and I found I was bathed in cold sweat. I took a hot shower and tried some prana-otani breathing exercises to calm my racing heart, but it took me more than an hour to fall asleep again.

The next morning we had to prepare for action. After a brief breakfast brought by room service, we went out; we had to get ourselves some arms: blasters, pistols, knives, and so on. Not that we would ever use them, but as drug dealers, we just couldn't be unarmed. Nobody would believe in our assumed new identity if we remained unarmed. Soon we were loaded with all kinds of deadly stuff, from poisoned throwing knives to micro-blasters. I felt very uncomfortable carrying all those things.

We went to the tavern to meet the Eryn. He was already there, his fur neatly combed from his eyes. Next to him sat a Broomak. His bones glistened in the dim light of the bar.

Behind him were two bodyguards, one Sylvan and one Tibbie, with their blasters ready to use at the shortest notice. I felt a chill running down my spine. The Broomak had piercing, glowing reddish eyes, and he was carefully watching our every move. We sat down on the opposite sides of the table and the negotiations started.

We told the Broomak that we were from the Ciegga system and were commissioned by the ruler of our system, Baron Kraak, to bring him a large supply of Sume. We said that our baron would like to receive a supply of Sume on a regular basis.

But about that arrangement, we said, we could talk only with The Boss of the whole organization. We said that the supply required was substantial and that the baron would pay in gold now or whatever currency would be most convenient for The Boss.

I looked at the Broomak over the table. There was doubt on his skeletal face. "Nobody can see The Boss!" he screeched. "I can make that deal for you," he insisted.

"No!" protested Migo. "We have our orders from the baron. We talk to The Boss, or there is no deal," he said firmly.

"If you are not cooperative, your organization might lose millions of credits," Hella teased him. "I wonder if your Boss will be happy about it when he finds out."

The flash of fear was clearly visible in the Broomak's eyes. "Well, I'll see what I can do," he said thoughtfully.

"Tell me where you are staying, and somebody will contact you when I have a word from The Boss. But I do not think that he will see you. He doesn't deal with anybody but his closest few assistants."

The Broomak got to his feet with an unpleasant clatter of his bony limbs. He nodded his bushy head to us and waved for his bodyguards to follow.

We got up too, leaving the dazed Eryn at the table. We decided that one of us would have to stay at the hotel at all times in case we were contacted. The nerve-wracking wait begun.

A few days passed. We had no word from The Boss. Maybe the organization somehow discovered that we weren't true drug dealers. I think we were being watched and followed in those next few days; the feeling of uneasiness grew stronger. I didn't like neither the place nor the situation, and I wished we didn't have to play games, dangerous games at that. There was nothing we could do but wait. We waited.

They came on the fifth night. We were sleeping in our hotel room when the door sprang open with an unpleasant creaking noise and a group of gloomy, nightmarish figures walked in. They must have had door lock deactivating devices.

I jumped to my feet and tried to gather my clothes together. From the corner of my eye, I saw Migo's surprised expression. A quick mind check assured me that at least Sparkie hadn't been caught unawares. He had hidden in the usual pocket of my coveralls, thank goodness.

Another group entered, bringing with them Hella from the adjoining room. She didn't resist them, knowing that we would probably be taken to The Boss, as we requested.

The leader of our visitors, a tall, gloomy Hesper with an ugly purple-violet wrinkled skin and almost vertically positioned slits for eyes, gave us two minutes to get ready.

I knew that we might not come back to the hotel

anymore. We went. A black, windowless Ardux waited outside. We took our seats and took off. Our flight wasn't too long. I tried to orient myself in the terrain mentally ... We were going southeast. We landed, and our escorts pushed us out, not too gently.

We were taken into a small building that looked like a storehouse of some kind. After a ten-minute walk, we finally reached our destination, a small room. There was a desk with some microfilms and holopictures on it. Behind the desk in a wide armchair, a strange creature sat.

It must have been some kind of a mutant, for I have never heard of a species that might look like that. We must have weighed at least 600 pounds. His skin was unpleasantly transparent, and we could see his blood vessels, veins and layers of fat tissue quite distinctly. It made me slightly nauseated. I made an effort to control the repulsion I felt.

We stood there watching him, transfixed. He was watching us, too, very, very carefully. I had a feeling that he was looking straight into my soul and I shut my mental barriers against this intrusion.

He waved at us to come closer. We did. There were no chairs for us to sit down -- we were to remain standing. I had the feeling he wasn't the person that we wanted to see; that it was a trick or a test. No, the creature before us wasn't The Boss. I was pretty sure of that. We were now only two yards from the mutant.

"Tell me about your mission here," he demanded.

We stood close together. I knew that my friends

perceived the same thing I did about our host.

"We want to see The Boss," said Migo firmly. "We will talk about our mission only with The Boss himself."

The mutant was looking at us angrily. "I am The Boss," he barked.

"No, you are not," said Migo steadily. "Please take us to The Boss. Do not waste our time. We can see through you. You are just one of The Boss's minor assistants."

There was a long moment of silence. I was getting frightened. What if the gangsters knew who we really were? I started perspiring and my hands shook, so I put them in my pockets to conceal the trembling.

After what seemed like an eternity, the mutant barked something to our escorts. I didn't know the dialect he used, but we were pushed out of the room and the door slammed behind us.

We were taken through countless dark passages, and up and down staircases. There must have been several levels underground. Then, at the end of the longest corridor I ever saw in my entire life, there was a small wooden door. It opened and we entered a dimly lit small room with star maps hanging on the walls.

There was a little, shriveled old man sitting behind an ordinary wooden desk. He wasn't even five feet tall and looked like a wizened ape. But there was an aura of power around him. I knew unmistakably that this was The Boss. There was no doubt about it.

We stopped before his desk and bowed our

heads before him. Since we had managed to get to the central figure in the organization, we were to proceed with step two of our plan.

Migo engaged The Boss in a conversation. I concentrated on sending mental messages to our ships waiting just beyond the orbit of Zolla. I made contact with the communication officer on duty. Each of us was equipped with a homing device. The ships locked on the subtle signals emitted by the devices and should have no trouble finding us. They were to move in at once. We just had to gain time and try to stay alive in the meantime. I wondered how long Migo would be able to hold The Boss's attention. The expert police crew of the ships would need about forty five minutes to find us. If we were discovered before that, we might be in real trouble.

I saw pearls of sweat on Migo's forehead. Was he running out of ideas? Hella scratched herself behind the ear nervously. And Sparkie? Where was Sparkie? He had left his hiding place and was nowhere inside. Oh, I wished I was somewhere else. I wished Princess Liss was with me. I wished...

The Boss suddenly struck his desk with his fist.

"I don't believe a word you're saying," he screeched. "Take them away," he yelled to the guards.

"But .. " I tried to save the situation. "You have only listened to my lieutenant, not to me. I am the one authorized to negotiate on the baron's behalf. There are other things he can offer you for the Sume, things of infinitely greater value than gold."

For a moment, I had caught The Boss's attention. He hesitated, halfway through motioning his guards to take us away, and I racked my brain for something to offer him.

Then I felt the power of The Boss's mind reaching into mine, and quickly slammed my mental doors.

Not quite fast enough. He might not know who we were, but he had learned enough to know we weren't who we said we were.

The Boss motioned to his guards. He had apparently had enough of us -- his greed overcome by his caution.

"Take them to our special treatment chamber. I want to know who they really are. What do they want here? I want an answer within the hour. Go!" The guards were trained to act quickly. They dragged us from the room.

We were disarmed in seconds. One of the escorts kicked me between the ribs, and a sharp pain shot through my rib cage. Would we survive this? I wasn't sure. It must have been about ten minutes since our signal. Could we survive another thirty five? The ships must have emerged from light speed and must be dropping fast toward the surface of Zolla. We had to hang on somehow.

Migo moaned gently. Our guards were handling us roughly. If I understood correctly, we were to be tortured to extract our true identities from us. I was terrified. I wasn't used to violence and pain and such an overwhelming malice.

We were brought into a large chamber with no windows. The place had very unpleasant vibrations. There were strange instruments hanging on the walls. When I examined them and guessed their purpose, my hair stood up in horror. It couldn't be possible. In our civilized universe, such an unspeakable, cruel things couldn't exit. And yet they did exist, before my very eyes.

Hella's smothered cry reached my ears. She was being forced into a small egg-shaped capsule. She could only fit in there shrunk into an uncomfortable embryo position. But in spite of her protests, she was squeezed inside the capsule and locked in there. The capsule started rotating with terrifying speed around the central pivot. Strange, violet zigzags of lightning, the explosions of some malignant energy, appeared on the surface of the capsule like cracks on an eggshell. The ether filled with Hella's silent, mental scream of suffering.

Meanwhile, I saw Migo tied to a large metal frame, each hand and leg locked into one of the four corners of it. Then the frame was hung over a large pool of a gaseous, foggy looking acid. One wrong move and Migo would dip into the deadly stuff. He desperately tried to balance his big body. I saw panic on my friend's face but I couldn't help him.

My guards grabbed me roughly and pushed me down. A strong kick landed on my rib cage. Another one dug into my kidneys. I have never been so humiliated in my life.

They put a spiky collar on my neck and led me on a chain leash around the room, kicking my back, laughing and having their horrid fun at my expense. Every time I tried to move, the spikes dug deeper into my neck, hurting me terribly. How long could I endure this treatment?

We had approximately twenty minutes left

before the police troops would land and come to our rescue. Where was Sparkie? My mind was racing. I had to do something. We intelligent citizens of the galaxy couldn't permit such things to happen. I still heard Hella's mental scream in my inner ear. Oh! What could I do? I called out to Sparkie, but he didn't answer. It was very difficult in the present situation, but I tried to send waves of positive feelings to our cruel guards. They still laughed and kicked me.

No, they were too far out in their cruelty to even hear me, or to react to my mental messages.

"Sparkie, damn it! Where are you?" Then, after a long silence, my friend popped out of thin air and circled over my head. He didn't sparkle because he didn't want to be detected. "Just about time," I complained in direct mind speech. "I thought that you would never come." I grumbled.

"I was just investigating the place, looking for the best ways out," he explained apologetically.

"Well, don't just hover there in midair. Don't you see our situation? Do something."

"Hmmm, what can I do? What can I do? Oh, yes, I know. But don't get scared, Dave, okay?"

"Just do something, quick!" I ordered.

Suddenly, with total surprise and horror, I noticed that my skin was covered with scales, my hands disappeared at my sides, and when I cried in horror, I issued a hissing sound.

Sparkie had changed me into a snake. My guards jumped sideways in terror, dropping the chain. I was free!

Once I realized Sparkie's plan, I instantly started

to play along with it. I hissed at our captors as venomously as I could. Since I was now a snake, without a neck, my spiky collar fell off.

"Okay, Sparkie! Good job!" I cried in my mind. "Now, let's free Migo and Hella, quick!"

We started with Migo, who had already touched the acid in places and had opened angry-looking wounds on his knees and elbows. I swung the frame from its deadly position over the pool of acid, and then Sparkie turned him into a big lizard with a high crest alongside his spine and tail. My only worry was that the bandits would sober up and simply shoot us. Luckily, they were so stunned, they gathered by the wall, whispering among themselves with fright. Good!

They probably thought that we must be powerful sorcerers or something of that sort. Hah!

Together with Migo, we stopped the fast-spinning capsule. When we opened the hatch, we found that Hella was unconscious. We dragged her out of her prison and tried to revive her. When she came around and opened her eyes, pale with suffering, she screamed, seeing a lizard and a snake leaning over her. We reassured her mentally that it was a disguise, an illusion. She sighed with relief.

We had no time to lose. I saw the bandits reaching for their weapons. They weren't going to let us go. Sparkie changed Hella quickly into a griffin -- a lion with wings.

She groaned, stretched her powerful body, flapped her wings, and flew at our opponents.

Several of them fired. Luckily they missed her and we moved to her rescue. I mentally perceived that the police troops had just landed, not too far from where we were now.

"Good," I thought. "They will be here soon."

Not soon enough, however. The enemy opened fire. They must have realized at last that our transformation was but an illusion, a trick. We all fell to the ground, trying to avoid the deadly beams from the enemy blasters. Sparkie dropped his illusion projection on us, and turned toward the enemy, trying to distract them.

We regained our real looks, and it felt good to be human again. I didn't have much time to enjoy it, however; we were under heavy enemy fire. We lay flat on the ground, hidden behind whatever cover we found to protect us. It was getting hot in the chamber from the energy discharges.

"Oh! Will we make it?" And then a thought struck me. I froze behind the solid rock square block which was protecting me from the enemy fire. Yes, it seemed so simple, but would it work? If not, I won't have time for regrets. I would be dead.

Well, it was worth trying. With deep prana-otani breathing, I started to fortify my body's bio-energetic field. I felt it growing stronger, denser, more substantial.

"It must work. It must," I prayed. Deep breathing took me into a trance. I kept repeating affirmations of invulnerability.

"I am the light. I am unconditional love. I am perfection. Whatever negative forces I encounter are only the result of my or others' imperfect thinking. Once I correct the way I think, I correct the situation. I am perfect. Everything around me is perfect. Whatever negative forces are there released around me, have no power over me. My bio-energetic field is impenetrable to any negative influence and will deflect the bullets and the energy charges. Nothing can touch me or hurt me. I am perfection."

I felt strong now; and my energy field felt almost as solid as the rock I hid behind. I stood up and stretched my hands out before me toward our oppressors.

The bandits stopped their fire for a while, confused. I came out from behind my shelter and moved slowly toward them. Regaining their senses, they fired straight at me. I walked toward them step by step. The beams of energy were bouncing off my invisible shield.

I saw confusion and disbelief on the faces of our opponents. It was a good thing they didn't know about my mind control and mind-over-matter stuff. I was only about three yards from them. They still kept firing at me with the full potential of their blasters, but I knew now that they couldn't hurt me, and they were terrified. They thought that I was some kind of a supernatural being instead of just a well-trained SNYX. That is a common reaction when such phenomena are not understood for what they really are.

Anyway, I was very close to them now. Seeing that they could not stop me, they dropped their weapons to the ground and ran. I laughed.

Migo and Hella rose from the floor, massaging their aching limbs.

"I thought for a moment that you had gone

mad," confessed Hella, with concern. "I'm sorry for doubting you."

Migo didn't say anything, but I saw that he was profoundly shaken. I embraced my friends and we waited for the police troops to come and do their part of the job.

About three hours later, it was all over. All the criminals had been caught and transferred to their cells on the starships. The Boss was among them. We had to identify him among hundreds of prisoners. He tried to erase the record of his operations and contacts from his main computer, but we managed to rescue enough to enable us to locate the Deyan hunters and paralyze their criminal, cruel activities. The slaughter of innocent Deyans had been stopped. Our mission had been accomplished.

We left all other matters, like taking care of the prisoners and bringing them to trial, in the expert hands of the police forces, and we returned to Teenpon.

I was to spend a week with Princess Liss on Snauru. Again, I felt like the happiest man in the universe. My friends, Hella, Migo and Sparkie, came along. They needed some rest before our twelfth and last assignment.

CHAPTER 24

This week with Princess Liss on Snauru was like a beautiful dream. We walked together, holding hands, kissed under the shade of the golden dragon trees, bathed in the enchanted springs in the sacred mountains, drank the elixir of ecstasy and made love in the Crystal Cave. We vowed to each other that we would always be together, that nothing was going to separate us -- ever. She told me about her father's plan to marry her to the Emperor of Godira, but she promised me to oppose those plans and wait for me.

When the time of her departure came, I felt as if part of me was torn from my very being. I had to do some really serious mind exercises to be able to function normally after she had gone home.

I didn't have much time to ponder over my emotional problems, however. Our next assignment came to our group almost like a sentence. There were reports of some serious disturbances in Cata Ronga System. There were always problems with the Furies. Yes, the Furies; the most dangerous and vicious creatures in the universe. My skin crept on my back at the mere thought of them. And now we were to go and face them, deal with them. I wasn't sure if I could cope with them. Please, anything but Furies!

We were approaching the Cata Ronga System. It was a vast star cluster spread over several hundred light years in space. When I looked at it from the distance, it reminded me of a clenched fist. I had a bad feeling about this trip. Hella, Migo and Sparkie were also worried, and we didn't talk much.

Many had faced the Furies and died. The odds were against us. Furies were expert killers. The most terrifying thing about them was that they could kill with a thought, without warning, without reason. I felt goose bumps all over my body. I could not control my fear. The star cluster was getting bigger and bigger on the front screen. Facing the Furies was inevitable. We were heading for Bataklan, a large blue star circled by eleven planets.

The report said that the fifth planet of the system ceased to exist, changing into a thick belt of meteorites. The planet called Xanthia used to be inhabited by the only human race in the entire Bataklan system. Now they were no more. We were to find out what caused this terrible disaster, and why. After all, whole planets were not supposed to disappear without the trace. Everybody suspected that it was doing of the warlike and cruel race of the Furies. The Furies were scattered throughout the whole star cluster. They were everywhere. On the red Gandarin and yellow Sednia and the violet dwarf star of Jaxinth.

My heart was beating fast as I watched the

screen. The Furies were close. I could sense them. We approached the meteorite belt, all that remained of the once beautiful planet of Xanthia. We took samples from some hundred asteroids, measured the radioactivity and electromagnetic currents, and checked the Ying-Yang polarity level. The radioactivity was very high. The electromagnetic currents formed chaotic whirlpools, and the Yin Yang polarity was way out of balance. We discovered a very serious disturbance on the subatomic level of the mineral probes. We fed all the results to our ship computer. After a careful analysis, we got our answers. The destruction of the planet had come about as a result of the careless manipulation of the planet's plasma on the subatomic level.

Careless or ignorant or intentional we didn't know. It happened as a response to highly increased negative vibrations, possibly caused by carefully directed and channeled thought forms emitted from the powerful source on Bantun, the neighbor planet of the system covered by a thick layer of clouds. I looked at the yellowish-orange atmosphere of planet Bantun on the screen, with a stunned expression. Was that possible -- that thought forms could blow up an entire planet?

I had learned before in the Academy that negative collective thought forms might cause serious changes on the surface of a planet, like earthquakes and volcanic eruptions, but to blow up the whole thing? I considered this thought in total disbelief. Could thought forms be so powerful as to alter the vibration of subatomic particles? Was it possible?

I looked at Migo, questioning. He was about as surprised as I was. Hella was sitting with her legs crossed nonchalantly, but in spite of her casual air, I sensed that she was deeply worried and disturbed, too.

"Well, seems like we will have to go to Bantun to check things out," postulated Migo.

"Yeah, this is probably the only way to figure out what is really happening here," I agreed.

"I hate to think about it, but the fact that they might have an emitter powerful enough to manipulate the entire planet, I find very disturbing," added Hella.

"Just think what it could do to our ship." Sparkie joined the conversation, hovering in mid-air right in front of the screen.

"Bantun is inhabited exclusively by the Furies," stated Migo gravely, and I shivered.

"I have a bad feeling about it," I grumbled. "I wish there was some other way to accomplish our mission. I do not feel much like facing these adorable creatures face to face," I added with dismay.

"But when you do, don't forget to hold onto your inner goodness and your sanity with all your strength. People have been known to lose their heads and our mental asylums are still full of them," said Hella. "Building up an extra mental body shielding might help. We should start to work on it every day,' she added.

"Perhaps you are right," Migo admitted. "We all have to prepare ourselves for the confrontation awaiting us very carefully."

"After all, not many survive an encounter with the Furies," Sparkie broke in, with such a note of fatalism that my throat tightened and tears filled my eyes.

The atmosphere of the desolate planet of Bantun was a dense layer of clouds varying in color from yellow to angry red. I could almost feel the resistance of the clouds against the sides of our starship. Our gravitational stabilizers were working at the maximum frequency, and still I could perceive a slight trembling of the ship, interrupted by stronger shudders from time to time.

We came out of the clouds at 5:35 standard time and circled the planet at low altitude, searching for the best landing spot. The Furies must have known that we came, as they have a very sophisticated radar tracking system, easily reaching the universal standards. But if they did know of our approach, they didn't do anything to prevent us from landing. Not yet, anyway.

The tightness in my throat persisted. I was really scared. The surface of the planet was a strange sight. It looked like something out of a bad dream. Most of the globe was covered with crystalline mountains in the wildest shapes one could imagine. They formed peaks and arches and the semi-transparent orange stone was like Swiss cheese, with the holes in it, forming tunnels and caves, filling all the interior of the mountains with passages. A real maze. That's where the Furies lived, in the large caves inside their ghastly mountains.

About one-third of the planet was covered with a yellowish ocean. Who knew what lived there? I wasn't sure I wanted to find out. In other words, the whole planet of Bantun was like a big ball of cheese in its structure.

"Dave." Migo interrupted my reverie. "We would like you to concentrate and tell us where that nasty annihilating beam comes from. We will land as close as possible to our target," he said.

"I don't think we would survive long if we had to traverse this enchanting landscape," sneered Hella, in her most sarcastic manner.

"Well, okay, give me a few minutes," I said. I relaxed in my seat and breathed deeply in and out for a while. I entered the trance state easily. I scanned the whole planet inside-out with my mind, searching, probing. I didn't at all like what I found.

There was a vast, shielded area deep under the surface of the planet, that I couldn't penetrate. The huge underground city was built around that area. That must be their capital, I thought. I had a feeling that the annihilator must be located in that shielded zone. The rest of the planet was full of little towns or settlements scattered here and there, where the Furies lived. They also lived in some of the underwater caves, I sensed.

There must have been several million inhabitants on Bantun. Since I couldn't penetrate the mystery of the heart of the capital, I came out of the trance and informed my friends of what I had found out. They didn't like it any more than I did.

We set our course for the capital. Nothing indicated that there was a big underground city here. I was amazed. Someone without the SYNX abilities would never find it.

We lowered our flights to just a few hundred yards above the ground and then landed in a nice circular spot between two sharp orange peaks. We had to use our suits and oxygen masks, as the atmosphere here was quite deadly for human beings. I wasn't surprised. After all, it was the land of the Furies what else can I tell you?

We armed ourselves as well as we could, our Gravi-T-belts fully functioning. Making sure that everything was working perfectly, we opened the hatch and went out, securing our ship with our strongest energy shield.

The ground felt strange under our feet. It was like stone, but at the same time I had a feeling that it vibrated in a strange manner. That resonation was highly disturbing.

"This place gives me the creeps," whispered Hella, using mind speech.

We walked toward one of the "holes", careful with every step we were placing on this strange, vibrating ground. Sparkie flew ahead of us to investigate. We moved forward slowly, carefully. I put my slightly shaking hands on my stunner. Its cold touch reassured me a little.

I felt uneasy. I was sick with uneasiness. Gee, what a place to be for a sensitive like me! It was killing me. My head was throbbing and I felt nausea rising in my throat.

Seeing the pale face of Migo, I knew that he didn't feel much better than I did. Hella's short hair stood up like the fur of an angry cat. The entrance to the maze was only yards away. We reached it and stood at the threshold.

"May the Light protect us," whispered Migo.

"May the Light be with us," whispered Hella, in a solemn voice.

"We are with the Light, always," I murmured, under my breath.

No matter what we would encounter, even the worst, we had to face it. Now. We moved on.

A few minutes later, Sparkie joined us.

"I saw them, I saw them!" He couldn't control his fear and excitement.

"Oh, boy, I have never seen anything like this in any dimension! Oh, I wish I never had to see them again! They are horrid! Cruel! Disgusting! Absolutely inconceivable!" chattered our friend, circling over our heads frantically.

"Okay, Sparkie, cool down." Migo tried to calm him.

"Try to make more sense. Tell us, how do they look? What do they do? Where are they? For goodness sake, control yourself and try to make a sensible report!" Hella scolded him.

We were standing in the middle of a wide corridor. There was an eerie orange-reddish semi-darkness surrounding us. Sparkie slowed himself down and lowered his pure energy force field. He sat on Migo's shoulder.

"Oh, goodness! How can I describe them! " cried Sparkie in consternation. "It is so difficult. They change all the time. From minute to minute, they are different. They are shape shifters. Yes, that's the right description for them. They express their thoughts in their shape, and in case you wondered, their thoughts are nasty. They know only anger and hate and cruelty. It gives them the most terrible appearance. They fight among themselves constantly. Their main occupation is to try to hurt each other. I don't think we stand a chance against them."

"Okay, Sparkie, get to the point," Hella interrupted him. "Do they have any weak points?"

Sparkie thought for a moment. I started sweating profusely under my suit.

"They are extremely vain creatures. They all want power, want domination. They would kill each other to gain it. They do it all the time. We have to be very careful, very, very careful." Sparkie fell silent.

We looked at each other uneasily. Well, it was our mission to go forth and solve the problem. There was no turning back.

We moved on. I was surprised that we hadn't been attacked yet. Or maybe we were walking into a trap. Maybe the Furies wanted to play the cat-and-mouse game with us before they killed us. I didn't know. We walked in silence. The vibration of the rock under our feet was getting stronger, more disturbing. The walls were full of smaller holes. There were strange, sharp, squeaking noises coming out of those openings. I hated to think what could have lived there.

The corridor was leading us down. We must have been about a thousand feet underground now. Soon we would be entering the city, I thought.

And then a different trembling ran through the

rock surrounding us, and we heard the Furies. It was the most terrifying, blood-freezing sound I have ever heard, something between a scream of terror and a horrible, demonic laughter. It was a chilling sound. My skin was covered with goose bumps.

"They're coming! They're coming!" cried Sparkie.

We grabbed our stunners and activated our shields. The tension was almost unbearable. Yes, they were coming. I could sense their approach. The particles of air around me vibrated with malice. I felt my legs turned into wool, and I was afraid I would faint.

Migo held his stunner in front of him with shaky hands. Even his eyes paled with fright. Hella braced herself and stood there with her feet parted for better balance, her stunner in her clenched hands. The black, star-like pupils of her eyes expanded and almost covered the golden radiant irises.

The vibration around us was getting stronger. The air was full of howling, laughing, terrifying, blood-freezing sounds. Sparkie plastered himself into my suit, trying to hide.

He was terrified too, even though he knew that they couldn't hurt him.

I had to lean my back against a wall, as my legs got so soft that I was afraid they wouldn't hold me upright anymore.

"May the Light be with me," I prayed.

The air around us exploded in cacophonic sounds. The Furies must have been able to emit ultra-sonics and sub-sonics, because I could feel a sound which was beyond our scale of hearing, a sound that hurt. I doubled up with pain. It was as though my flesh was being ripped from my bones. My stomach was like a furnace of evil fire. I had a tight knot in my throat and I couldn't scream. I sank to my knees.

How foolish it was to come here like this, unprotected, I thought weakly. I was already only semiconscious when I saw them -- the Furies. Oh, yes, they deserved their name.

They had earned it, several times over.

They sprang at us from all directions at once, from the corridor in front of us and from behind. And since they could easily change their shape, they also came through smaller holes in the walls and the ceiling.

I dropped my stunner to the ground. There was no use for that. The foul smell hit my nostrils. I closed my eyes, awaiting the Furies' deadly touch on my body. I shrank in anticipation. I heard Hella's smothered cry. Migo, next to me, was breathing in short, fast, labored breaths, with the accompanying hissing sound.

Then the impact came. The touch of the Furies on my body was like a high voltage electric shock. An excruciating pain exploded through my entire nervous system and it flooded my brain like a lightning bolt of malignant light. I realized that I was dying. "May the Light… May the Light ..." I tried to whisper, but the blackness revolved around me, and I was no more.

When I came around, I wasn't sure whether I was dead or alive. At first I thought that I had died, left my body, and was now in a free spirit state. It wasn't too bad. But then the pain came and I realized that I was still alive. I wished I wasn't. My whole body hurt terribly. I somehow had difficulty breathing, and my head was on fire with sharp, blinding pains shooting through my brain from time to time.

I tried to open my eyes. I couldn't see anything at first, but then I realized that through narrowed slits before my eyes, I could glimpse something. I touched my head. I had some kind of helmet on. It felt metal to the touch. And the picture before my eyes was funny somehow. I couldn't understand it. After a while, a recognition came. I was seeing things upside down.

I tried to move my legs. No way. They were bound in something solid and hard. I was simply hanging upside down, suspended in the air by my feet. My hair rose in horror. I tried to move my head sideways and see through the slits in the helmet if my friends were anywhere nearby.

I glimpsed Migo to my right. His face was red and his eyes bulging, as far as I could see through his helmet. Hella, to my left, was hanging limp and lifeless.

"Oh, no! She couldn't!" I cried in my mind to her.

"Hella! Hella! Hear me! Give me a sign that you are alive. Please, Hella!"

Slowly, very slowly, she came out of the oblivion.

"Dave?" came her weak answer. "Oh, Dave, what a mess we got ourselves into." She understood the situation in one flash of recognition. "And look at this awful place! Creepy, don't you think?"

Hella never lost her sarcasm, not even in the most dangerous situations.

"So, how in a thousand black holes are we going to get out of this?" she asked, trying to move her head left and right with an enormous effort, analyzing the place.

We were in a huge cave. It was dimly lighted, dull, yellowish-orange. Something that reminded me of stalactites and stalagmites protruded from the top of the cave where we were hanging and also from the ground. Sharp spikes sticking out threatened to spear anything unfortunate enough to fall upon them.

The Furies were nowhere in sight. That was a relief.

The upside-down position I was in was very uncomfortable. Blood was pulsating in my temples and I found it hard to concentrate.

And where is Sparkie? I thought. I had to get hold of myself. I had to analyze the situation carefully. There must be some way out. There simply must.

Deep, controlled breathing calmed down my wildly racing mind. First thing, where are we? I thought. Inside or outside the shielded city area? I expanded my mind outward, probing, questioning. The city was huge, full of hostile Furies. Their negative vibrations affected me terribly, causing an almost physical pain. How can we ever escape those nasty beings? It's a miracle that they let us live this long anyway. I tried to ignore the negative interferences, and kept probing.

Yes, we were now inside the shielded area. Not too far away from our cave, there was a place that I perceived as an enormous vortex of negative energies. I was dismayed by the power and malignant magnitude of it. Yes! That must be the deadly emitter, the annihilator we were sent here to find and disable or destroy.

Our target located, I searched for Sparkie. He was nowhere, as far as I could see with my mind's eye. I went a little deeper into the trance and tried again. He must be somewhere! And then I heard him cry, far, very far away, as if he was trapped in another parallel dimension.

"Dave . ..! Dave ... ! Run if you can! Get away from here as far as you can ... ! I am trapped ... ! You cannot help me...! Run!" His voice drifted away.

A cold shiver ran up and down my spine. What had happened to our friend? He needed our help! But what could I do? I was trapped myself. A prisoner. What could I do?

I linked my mind with Migo and Hella.

"Any suggestions?" I asked, with hope that they would come up with a plan.

"Could you check what is the nature of this vortex that can annihilate an entire planet?" requested Migo with practicality.

"When we know its nature maybe we can affect it or reverse its flow or something…" he postulated.

"Yes, that's a good idea," Hella approved. "I cannot think of anything else we could do at the present time," she added.

I wished I could free myself from this damned helmet. It was bothering me, breaking my concentration. The moment I thought of it, the lightning bolt of pain shot through my head, and I could almost see my grey brain cells sizzle. My vision clouded. Through the haze I could see the Furies coming. They flew into the cave and circled us, hanging there in the middle, watching us, talking in an unpleasant, screeching manner among themselves and laughing in that chilling way that made me shrink in panic.

There were a dozen of them. They were hideous. There couldn't possibly be any more terrifying creatures in the entire creation. The Universal consciousness must have miscalculated here somehow, must have made a mistake, I thought, watching them in utter terror, in utter panic. And yet, on the other hand, if they existed, there must be a purpose to it. If I couldn't see it at this very moment, that didn't mean that there wasn't one.

One of the Furies flew very close to me and peered through the slits in my helmet. I stopped breathing. Paralyzed with fear, I was watching as the creature stretched its long tentacles, pressed something on the side of the helmet, and removed it gently from my head.

I was now face-to-face with the Fury. It was terrifying, changing constantly into the most unimaginable shapes; it made me dizzy. And yet, there was something in those eyes, located on the very top of its head that made my heart jump. Maybe it was just the way I was brought up in the

Academy, conditioned to love all the creatures in the entire universe unconditionally. Or maybe there really was this spark of humanity in those otherwise terrifying eyes.

I couldn't help myself. I sent a feeling -- a thought -- of love toward my opponent, enveloped him with light and love.

A shiver ran through the Fury's body. He was like a dog shaking the drops of water from his fur after a swim. Did I really touch him? The other Furies, however, didn't like this exchange of feelings.

"Watch out, Dave," cried Hella alarmingly.

It was high time. One of the other Furies flew straight at me, changing his tentacles into sharp claws. I somehow managed to curl up and avoid this attack. My Fury, as I now thought of him, seemed,to argue with the others. Was he defending me, or insisting that "they kill me" immediately? I tried to listen on the mind speech frequency, trying to understand what was going on.

"Yukter! You are out of your mind!" cried the Furies.

"We must kill them all right away before they spread this strange disease among us," they insisted.

My Fury, called Yukter, didn't agree with the rest.

"No, we should not kill them!" he argued. "They might still be valuable to us," he insisted.

"Valuable? Hah! They have no value to us. Kill them!

Kill them now! Or better yet, let's feed them into the vortex.

"Yes, yes, let's do it!" they all agreed with excitement.

Yukter had been greatly outnumbered. His companions ignored his protests.

The cave filled with their shrill cries. "To the vortex with them!" they screamed.

I saw that Yukter didn't agree fully with his colleagues, but he didn't oppose them either. After all, he was a Fury himself. What could I expect from him? To rescue me? I didn't have the time for any more reflections. I felt the Furies' awful touch on my body.

They grabbed us and, releasing us not too gently from the rings holding our feet imprisoned, they carried us away. They almost dropped Migo.

"Damn those aliens. They are so clumsy, they can't even fly," they complained, catching him halfway to the floor full of spiky stalagmites. For a moment, I thought that this was the end of our friend.

I was carried by three fearful specimens who held me suspended among themselves. Are they taking us where Sparkie is imprisoned? I speculated. Out of the corner of my eye, I could see Hella hanging limp among her escorts. She had been resisting them, and they had sent her some kind of energy shock which knocked her unconscious. Oh! I hope they didn't kill her, I prayed.

We left the cave. We were carried now through a high arched dark passage where strange wind currents raged. Even the Furies had difficulty making their way here. There were charges of electricity in the air. I could feel rather than hear a strange humming filling the whole space around us. It was very unpleasant. I started sneezing and my skin itched and prickled. Am I allergic to Furies, or perhaps their vortex? The funny idea crossed my mind.

In a little while, I wouldn't need to worry about such things anymore. In a little while, we would all be dead.

But Sparkie was alive. The hope awakened in me. Was it due to his pure energy state? I couldn't find an answer for that question at that moment. Soon enough we would learn. Very soon. We were being carried from one dark corridor to another.

Then we passed through a huge, hollow space where the settlements of the Furies was located. It was a very weird city. There were dark, foreboding openings in the walls of this enormous cavern.

"That's where they live, probably." I thought.

The Furies were flying back and forth, screeching at each other; some were fighting. still others were in the process of consuming their freshly killed enemies. Several half-eaten carcasses were hanging from the top of the cavern, emanating the most disgusting smell that ever hit my nostrils. Furies were without doubt the cruelest creatures in the Universe.

Other caverns similar to that one followed, then we entered a maze of corridors. The stench wasn't so bad here. Our captors holding us in their firm grip were moving fast through the labyrinth of the passages.

I felt the vortex very close now. All my body

hair was standing up as if electrified.

Then all of a sudden we flew out of the dark, gloomy corridor and the bright light hit our eyes. My lids dropped automatically to protect my sensitive eyes from it.

After a moment, from under the veil of my lashes, I glimpsed the whole picture. We had been brought to a place so huge that it must have been reaching deep into the core of the planet. I couldn't even see the ceiling of the hall. In the middle of the place, a huge pillar of angry looking violet light was turning round and round. I couldn't see neither the beginning nor the end of the pillar, so enormous it was, stretching endlessly downward and upward.

"This must be the deadly beam, the annihilator of planets we were looking for," I thought. "And now we found it. But so what?" We were powerless to do anything to gain control over it. What's worse, we would soon be a part of it, feeding it with our life energies. It was about the most terrible end I could have imagined: to contribute my life energies to the forces of evil.

The Furies were flying closer to the vortex. The sweet face of Princess Liss flashed in my mind. "Oh, Liss, help me!" I cried out into the ether. "Liss, I will die soon! Liss, my love! Help me! Liss!!! "

Things started happening so quickly then that for a while I couldn't comprehend them. I saw Migo's big body flying into the vortex, and then Hella's. They were immediately swallowed by the turning flame. Only a few sparks flew where my friends disappeared in its fiery embrace. Now it was my turn. I felt the Furies release me and launch me into the hellish fire.

"Liss!" I screamed, and closed my eyes in anticipation of being burned into cinders.

To my surprise, the fire was cold, very cold. It penetrated all my cells, ate through the bones, through my brain. It paralyzed me, froze me. I was falling down, turning, and tumbling.

I felt my reason leaving me as if my mind was dissolving like an ice cube in hot water. "Goodbye, Liss," I cried with the last stroke of my will, and then the darkness closed upon me. I was no more. I ceased to exist. I reached the end.

"Why can't I be left alone?" was my first semi-conscious thought. "After all I went through, don't I deserve a little peace after I die?" But then, I wasn't dead, was I? No, my body was frozen to the bone, my mind was weak, but I was alive all right.

Somebody was trying to catch my attention. I felt a nagging somewhere at the back of my mind. I was overcome with such lethargy that I couldn't be bothered. But the nagging was getting stronger.' "Dave! Dave?" I perceived a call.

"Liss ?!" I was awake all of a sudden. "Liss, is it really you?" I couldn't believe my luck. Did she really hear my call through thousands of light years of space? Was it the power of our love that made it possible?

"Yes, Dave, it's me!" came an answer from far away.

"You have to concentrate now," she instructed. "You can still win. Go to the source of the vortex. You might be able to reverse its flow. Go! "The sweet voice of Liss drifted away.

"Liss! Liss!" I called, but there was no reply. What did she say I could do? To go to the source of the vortex?

How? Where is it? I thought, in total confusion. But slowly, as I calmed down, I started thinking more clearly. A simple plan emerged. Of course, she was right. Why hadn't I thought of it before?

I consequently went through a ritual prana-otani breathing to achieve a trance state. When I was ready, I expanded my mind outward, searching. Suddenly, a clear picture came into my mind. In a strange, dim cave, a group of Furies, some twelve of them, hovered around a huge, reddish crystal. It was suspended in the air and emanated its own malignant purplish light from within. The Evil stone!

I recognized it immediately. I never thought that Evil stones still existed. They were all supposed to be destroyed thousands of standard years ago when the Galactic Council overthrew the old feudal regime. And yet it was an Evil stone all right; I was sure of that.

It had to be destroyed, at no matter what cost. It had created the vortex. It had annihilated the neighbor planet. It had to be terminated.

But where was I, by the way? I had no sense of my body at all. Was my flesh destroyed in the cold fire? I pushed this thought aside. I would worry about my body later on, I decided firmly. For what I had to do now, I didn't need it anyway.

I started to prepare myself for a final confrontation. As I went deeper into the trance and relaxed, I sensed the presence of my friends in spirit form. That was enough encouragement for me. We linked our minds: Migo, Hella, Sparkie and me, and then together called out to the Light and Higher Consciousness to aid us.

As we meditated on the highest realms, the incredible, invincible force rushed through our minds, and it nourished them. We had it at our disposal now. It made me feel like a powerful giant. Together we moved our unified beam of Light Force toward the crystal.

Even the Furies couldn't stop us now. They flew around the crystal frantically, but couldn't prevent the forces of Light from surrounding and penetrating it. Purple lightning shot from within the stone, aiming at us. In our disembodied, pure consciousness state, it couldn't hurt us. A deep angry rumbling ran through the crystal, through the whole cave, through the entire planet.

The crystal shuddered and exploded into a million violet sparks. The malignant force 'of the stone was released, hit us, and swept us away. The light filled my mind suddenly.

At least we destroyed it, I thought triumphantly. It was my last thought.

Six months later, on Teenpon, we were finally ready to leave the clinic. There was nothing much that remained of our physical bodies after the confrontation with the vortex, and we had to have them regrown from scratch in the regeneration tanks. But as I look at myself now, I think I like my new body even better than the old one. I am somewhat taller and better looking now.

Migo, for the first time in years, is slim and trim, and Hella is even more beautiful than ever before. All thanks to Sparkie. We all owe him our lives. He saved us from the terrible blast of the evil forces, whatever was left of us, that is. And here we were as good as new, getting ready for our promotion.

Princess Liss promised me to come to Teenpon especially for the celebration. We had successfully completed all twelve of our Herculean tasks, and were now to be promoted as fully grown and responsible citizens of the Galactic Union. We were very proud of ourselves. After all, it wasn't easy to get where we were now. Though we had some fun during our tests, too.

I hoped that now it would be permitted for Liss and me to be together. Well, I would talk to her about it, when I saw her in a week's time. For now, I just wanted-to share with you my satisfaction and the deep conviction that there is no way that the forces of the Darkness can ever win over the forces of Light and Love we all carry in our hearts.

Remember! No matter what happens to you, THERE IS ALWAYS A WAY OUT.

CHAPTER 25

Many years have passed since the time of my promotion, many long years. As a reward for having such positive results during my tests, I was appointed to a high honor. I became Assistant to the Governor -- the President of the Galaxy.

The time came to do some serious work. Migo had been appointed the head of the Institute for Energy Research. There he will be able to fully employ his genius in scientific research.

Hella was sent to the General Development Office on Elaria to work on the planning and development of the new worlds and planets. She was very happy with this assignment.

It was what she always wanted to do, but she was a little sad that we had to separate. We assured her that we would be dropping by Elaria any time we were in the neighborhood.

Then, finally, Sparkie became the captain of an intergalactic starship. He, being a pure energy being, unlimited by flesh, could operate and navigate the whole ship himself, in cooperation with the ship's computer, of course.

We will not be able to see him often, as voyages to the farthest corners of the universe take long years, even at the speed of light. But our bonds of love and friendship will always be strong between us, and it will not change, no matter how many light years of empty space separate us.

My duty as the Governor's assistant was to travel to old systems and planets where some political problems had arisen. I was a mediator, a peace-bringer. It wasn't an easy job, but after each successful mission, when peace was brought back between some warring nations or planets, I felt great satisfaction, and the Governor was very happy with my work. I was promoted to be his general assistant, his right hand.

In all those years, Princess Liss never left my side. Yes, she obtained, with some difficulty, permission from her father to leave her official post in the government of O'Venti, and we were married with all the proper ceremonies on Rajpeeti. The Governor himself blessed our union.

We have been very happy together since then. Liss went with me on all my missions, and was my support and best advisor through difficult times. The more we knew each other, the stronger the bond of our love was. She never regretted her decision.

We lived in a nice house, very close to the Governor's mansion. The years went by.

And now, I will tell you about this special assignment, as it proved to be a turning point in my entire career. I was sent on a peace mission. The moment I embarked on my diplomatic starship, course for Amerronda System, I knew, or rather felt, that it was going to be a difficult mission.

Liss, by my side, only squeezed my hand, as if guessing my thoughts.

Soon we were in our reserved suite. Since the voyage would take a whole three months, we had to have a place to stretch. We settled into our temporary home. My two secretaries had been lodged next door, so they would always be at hand when I needed them.

I had a lot of work to do during this trip. I had to carefully prepare myself for the coming confrontation.

And now, let me tell you about my mission. There had been reports to the General Governor's office of dangerous political unrest between two large neighbor star systems -- Amerronda and Sovidjan. Both were inhabited by intelligent races, Amerronda by a highly sophisticated caninae race of Amernais and Sovidjan by the advanced feline race of Cill'Baj. Both were highly developed. They had been in a state of cold war for many years now, threatening to explode in a devastating nuclear disaster at any time. The citizens of both systems lived in continuous fear of holocaust and destruction.

Both sides were spending millions of credits on more and more sophisticated, more deadly weapons, thinking that it was the only way to secure their peace. They both had this silly conviction that the more killing bombs and weapons they had in their possession, the safer and more invulnerable they were. The arms race between Amerronda and

Sovidjan had reached a dangerous level, and the Galactic Government had to do something about it before they blew each other up, blinded in their folly.

Outside help was needed. It was my job to make the nations see how pointless it was to build more weapons. Because the ridiculous side of that situation was that neither of them could ever use it. The moment one missile was sent from either side would mean a devastating nuclear war. Sending this missile would be suicide for the one who did it. The antimissiles would be sent from the other side immediately, and the originator of the missile-sending would be annihilated, together with millions of innocent civilian inhabitants on his planet, peaceful beings who, for the most part, didn't agree to the building of the weapons. And aggressive politics of their government in the first place.

We couldn't let that happen. The arms race had to be stopped at once, and understanding should be brought to the governments of both systems.

I sighed and lowered the report I was reading to the desk. I was tired. I felt Liss's warm hands go around my neck. Well, perhaps there will be enough time to worry about two warring nations later. Now, I have much more pleasant things to do, I thought.

I felt Liss's warm, soft lips on mine. Her green dress, made of some kind of shimmering fabric, clung to her shapely body like a second skin. I put my arms around her waist and pressed her to my chest. I soon forgot Amerronda and Sovidjan, and practically everything else. There would be time to worry about them later. For now, I had better things to occupy my time.

We landed on Amerronda and were transferred to the capital of the system, Farrington. We were to have an audience with President Sardori in a couple of days. Meanwhile, we settled into a comfortable villa put at our disposal by the government.

Having some free time, we decided to take a look around to get a better picture of the situation. A small planet-hopper took us all around. The ship's computer was programmed to give us information and sightseeing tips. We really enjoyed this trip. Liss liked the spectacular waterfalls of Siagra best. I liked the ocean and the nice little oceanside towns of Halisfornia.

The standard of life was quite high in this system. The Amernais, the inhabitants of the system, were very pleasant caninae beings of a few different races and sizes, varying from the size of a big, six feet tall human being to the size of a small cocker spaniel dog.

There was a lot of vice and violence here, though. It was the fear and insecurity of the citizens, exploding and clashing in a violent manner with the law of the system.

Yes, it was definitely an expression of fear.

The society was also very commercialized. Millions of the Amernais, sitting for hours every day glued to their personal VVD screens, were fed with all kinds of cheap stuff, like criminal adventures and violence-promoting pictures. I wondered how, having such a wonderful system of broadcasting, they didn't transmit something more valuable, that would help the citizens to better understand themselves and the world around them, and eventually change it for the better. It was a paradox that I couldn't solve.

I made my notes. All this I would discuss with the President. It was vital to my peace mission to stress the necessity to heighten the awareness of the citizens of Amerronda.

We came back to Farrington for the meeting with the President.

Grell Sardon was a tall, strong Amernais of a regal appearance. There was an aura of incredible personal power around him. I liked him at once. I realized that he might prove a little stubborn, though. Our official talks took place in the White Tower, and then Liss and I were invited for an unofficial dinner. Liss was wearing her best white gown embroidered with pearls and brilliant T-stones. I was really proud of her as she charmed everybody and made everyone feel good and relaxed. This ability was one of her greatest gifts, apart from beauty and wisdom, that is.

In the next couple of days, I had more meetings with the President. Then we discussed and planned a meeting with the head of the Sovidjan system, to take place a month from now on the neutral ground of the planet Ramatishi. The President agreed that he, several of his ministers, and a group of representatives from different groups of citizens, backgrounds, and regions -- a representation of Amerronda system of about two hundred beings -- would attend the peace conference on Ramatishi.

I was glad. The first part of my mediator's mission had been accomplished.

We took off for Sovidjan. After two weeks on

the starship, we finally landed on the snow-covered planet of Sovidjan IV, the main planet of the whole system.

We were transferred to Kremos, the capital. Here the political atmosphere was entirely different. We weren't permitted to travel freely around the system. A serious escort had been appointed to us and we practically couldn't step outside our residence without him.

There was a whole army of bodyguards. Were they to guard us from the people, or the people from us? I wasn't entirely sure. Anyway, we were surrounded here by an aura of suspicion and mistrust. Or was I simply imagining things in my super-sensitive manner?

The meeting with a grave First Secretary and the head of the local government, Kim Gudanow, took place in a large audience room of the ancient palace of the long-dead kings of this realm. It was full of splendor. There were not many places in the universe where you could see such riches.

Once we started our talks, Kim Gudanow turned out to be a lot more pleasant than I had originally expected him to be. He was a chunky, wiry, striped yellow and ginger representative of a Cill'Baj race, a tiger-like being, with short, round ears and deep green shifty eyes. When I looked into those eyes, I felt a shiver running up and down my spine. I couldn't read him at all. I didn't know – I couldn't guess -- what his true intentions were.

Another thing bothered me. He and an army of his Cill'Baj assistants never smiled. I don't know if smiling and otherwise expressing your joy in life was forbidden in this realm, but even if it was the case, I couldn't prevent myself from doing so.

We had several meetings, official dinners, and more talk. We seemed to agree to the plan of meeting the delegation from Amerronda on Ramatishi, but there was this air of mistrust, suspicion, and constant readiness to counter-attack about the Cill'Baj we were dealing with. It almost seemed like an obsession. I couldn't very well relax in this atmosphere. That I made them agree to attend the conference was good enough at this time.

It was considered a great favor that we were invited to spend the weekend in Gudanow's private estate in the countryside. The temperature there was so low that we were provided with thick furs to wear. I was very opposed to wearing the skins of killed animals on my back, killing being absolutely forbidden in our part of the galaxy. In spite of my protests, reluctance and disgust, I was forced to wear it.

Gudanow's estate was truly impressive. His wife, a small, chunky tigress, like Cill'Baj, tried to do her best to entertain us, but I welcomed with true relief, the hour of our departure from Sovidjan. I longed to be in a brighter, more optimistic world.

Surely Ramatashi was optimistic enough, its blue mountains, with their peaks bathed in the mists; its sapphire, majestically rolling ocean; its big yellow sun, reminded me very much of a long-lost world, Earth.

I felt almost at home here. I liked that feeling, and Liss liked it too. We spent a wonderful week cruising the oceans of Ramatishi on the luxurious, floating island of Grisbane. It was like a second honeymoon. Besides pleasure, I had to do some work, however. I had to prepare myself for a final confrontation of the two opposing systems, and I had to bring them together somehow, build a bridge of understanding between them, end the dangerous and pointless struggle between them.

How exactly I was going to do it, I didn't yet know, but I didn't worry. I knew the right solutions would surface when the time came. They always did. Meanwhile, I enjoyed the sunshine and the swims in the clear, warm lagoons, and I listened to the tropical birds singing, and I felt happy.

I was happier still when Liss told me that she was expecting a baby, our first child. I was so proud that I almost burst with joy. She said it was going to be a boy, and it would be born in five months time. I couldn't wait to see it -- my own child.

It was a wonderful week, filled with joy and happiness. But good times such as this never last too long. The conference was to take place at Sorra, the capital of Ramatishi.

The representatives of the united Worlds had already taken care of the basics, like security and lodging for the delegates. The conference was open to any nation which would like to attend, so we could expect quite a crowd here, since the Amerronda-Sovidjan conflict was well known throughout the galaxy. Many nations worried about its outcome. The war, once unleashed, could spread and endanger other systems.

Finally the day came when the delegation started arriving. Sorra's main starport could hardly handle the rush. Intelligent creatures of almost every known species, race and shape came to witness the outcome of the peace conference.

I was getting a little nervous now. What if I wasn't able to convince them? What if I failed the Governor? What if the parties won't agree to mediate?

I started having nightmares. Liss had to wake me up in the middle of the night when I was tossing around the bed feverishly. Sometimes I was awakened by my own scream. I was almost relieved when the delegation of Amerronda arrived in Sorra on the first day of the local national holiday.

It was a celebration of life, and the beginning of a new season.

Grell Sardon was sitting by my side on the dais, watching the local festivities. He was a truly regal creature, with light brown fur a little faded with years, but his dark brown mane was still rich and thick. His deep hazel eyes shone with inner strength and wisdom.

A new hope entered my heart. Yes, this being should listen to reason, and if convinced, should act, considering the best interests of the citizens of his system. But would he be permitted to act? It was a known fact in the history of Amerronda that certain powerful representatives having to do with economy and investments in this system were very influential, at times going to the point of getting rid of a President who dared to act against their interests.

Therefore, the top security specialists had been employed to guarantee that nothing of that sort would happen here.

Now we waited for the delegation from Sovidjan. They were the last to arrive, just two days before we were scheduled to start the conference. Perhaps they waited to make an impressive entrance, I don't know.

Kim Gudanow, at the head of the delegation of three hundred beings, arrived in a golden starship, grave and serious as usual. We made every effort to make the situation more relaxed, but our latest guests clung stubbornly to their super-formal manners, and there was nothing we could do to make them relax. We made them as comfortable as we could, but it didn't seem to affect their attitude in the least.

The security men had their hands full. There were a few unsuccessful attempts to kill Grell Sardon. The attackers must have had self-destruct orders in case of being caught, because they all mysteriously died before they could actually be questioned. We doubled the bodyguards and kept our eyes open and our fingers crossed that they would prove quick enough to prevent any serious trouble.

Finally, the first day of the conference arrived. The huge conference hall was filled to capacity. The representative of the United Worlds, an old Saurian from Belonte, opened the debates. While he was greeting the representatives of thousands of star systems, I scanned the hall in amazement. Seeing so many beings, so many ways for nature to express herself, always filled me with awe. It made me feel proud and humble at the same time.

After the opening, it was my turn to speak. I rose to my feet and cleared my throat. My face filled the huge screen above, so everyone of the spectators could see my every move, my every expression.

I caught a glimpse of Liss sitting in the first row, right in front of the podium, and I immediately felt better.

"Dear friends," I started informally, "I am proud to see you all here gathered to witness a peacemaking agreement between two opposed star systems. The Governor would be proud, too, if he could be here with us. He sent me to act as his voice. You must all realize how important it is to maintain peace in our galaxy at all times. To live in peace is the right of all of us."

"If we are deprived of this right, our lives acquire a negative aspect. Fear kills our creative abilities, and we cannot develop and function to our full potential. This is an unforgiveable waste."

"Even if some of you live the greatest part of your lives suppressed, do you want your children to grow in the same environment? Don't you want to see your children happy and trusting instead of scared, intimidated and suspicious? If we don't act now, we might deprive our children of a happier, better life. We all must take the responsibility for what is happening, because it is directly or indirectly a result of our actions. Even apparently insignificant people without influence -- carpenters and mechanics and delivery men -- they are also responsible. How? They see the wrong around them, but they accept it and don't protest and don't object to it. That way, they leave the opportunity for the wrong to thrive."

I knew that my speech was transmitted to Amerronda and Savidjan and hundreds of other systems. I paused for a second, drawing a deep breath into my lungs.

"The moment we all take the responsibility for what is happening, we already take the first, and a very important step, toward change, toward peace. The next step, however, is even more important. The next step is to learn to express love."

A murmur ran through the hall. I heard the audience shifting on their seats uneasily. Someone in the back row laughed. I waited until everything quieted down and then I resumed my speech.

"Yes, my friends, I see surprise and disbelief on many faces. I mean what I just said. If you master love, you are much more powerful than if you had an arsenal full of deadly weapons and a handful of nuclear bombs. You then have the power to change without hurting, to heal instead of killing."

"Unconditional love is the highest law in our universe, and even if a few systems here and there still choose to oppose it, it won't be long before they will be reunited with the rest. I hope that they won't blow themselves up before that happens."

"Search your hearts, my friends. Deep down there, you know that what I just said is true. If you feel it and recognize it, now you should start acting accordingly. If you expect changes in your systems, you should start those changes on the personal, individual level, for that's where all the problems originate. Changes have to start within your hearts and from there spread wider and wider until every aspect of your life changes for the better. Just imagine, if those who just attempted to murder President Sardon acted according to the law of love, they would have never committed that act and lost their lives in the process. If those who build the deadly missiles realize how much damage and pain they can cause by constructing those weapons, and they stopped what they were doing, recognizing the wrongness of it, we wouldn't have to talk about peace today."

"You have the power to create your own peace, my friends. You can create peace and plenty instead of fear and insecurity. By the way, if all those credits that are spent on weapons were spent on the good of the country and of the citizens, on education and scientific research, and help for the poor, to name a few causes, yours would be thriving and you would live on a much higher level. Your planets would be changed into Gardens of Eden, where your every wish could be fulfilled."

"Think about it, my friends. Your future and the future of your children lie in your hands. Make the right choice."

There was a moment of silence after I finished my speech. After that, the whole place exploded with applause. Some of the assembled got up and others followed.

President Grell Sardon slowly rose to his feet, brushing back his rich mane, and joined in the applause. The whole delegation of Amernais followed. I could see that all participants were full of enthusiasm.

I looked at the delegation of Sovidjan. Kim Gudenow was scratching himself behind the ear with consternation. Hesitation shone in his green cat's eyes. All the delegates of Sovidjan were sitting as if on hot coals, unsure what to do, knowing that the eyes of the millions of beings all across the universe were directed toward them. They knew that they had to make a decision.

Yet Kim Gudenow didn't move. They were troubled. The applause was getting stronger, more insistent. I even heard whistles from the crowd. Some more aggressive beings from the audience yelled something toward the Sovidjanians, but it was drowned in the noise.

The tension in the hall was getting stronger. I was already afraid that if the Sovidjanians didn't join, we might have some serious problems here. Finally, however, the First Secretary, Kim Gudenow, rose to his feet and clapped his paws.

All his delegation of three hundred souls followed with eagerness and relief. I even thought that I noticed a trace of a smile on Gudanow's face, but then, I could be wrong.

No! I wasn't wrong. Unlikely as it might sound, he actually smiled. With a little practice, he might even learn to laugh.

Pride filled my heart. I realized that in spite of all the differences, anger and hate between Amerronda and Sovidjan, the first steps had been made toward understanding, toward peace, toward a better future. And the pride I saw on Liss's face, as she stood in the first row clapping her hands, was one of the best rewards I could imagine.

I thought of my future son, and I was glad that I was bringing him to a universe which is constantly improving, and I was proud and grateful for being given a chance to work toward this improvement.

Several days of debates passed. After the ice was broken the first day, the talks were now more relaxed, more sincere. I could see both sides really tried to reach an agreement, and worked with hope that they could indeed change things for the better.

It was difficult to let go of their old ways of thinking. It was not easy to let go of fear, which had been their constant companion until now. To replace this fear with love and trust, when they had lived all their lives in mistrust, was difficult.

Yet I could see changes slowly taking place. I knew that it would take long years to disarm both systems, change their economic structures and, what's more important, to do the reorientation of their citizens. Many things might go wrong in the process. Problems might arise, but any problem can be overcome, any wrongness corrected, if those participating are beings of good will. And I think that is what we all are; we just might get misled every once in a while and wander off the path of love, but once we see that we are lost, we should remember what the right path is, and return to it immediately.

There were a few days dedicated to rest from debates, filled with celebration and merry-making. We wanted both delegations to mingle to get to know each other on a more personal level, to exchange thoughts and ideas.

It worked. After this intermission, the

agreements were easier to accomplish. We didn't expect, however, that the conference would take a very dramatic turn towards its end.

Finally the day came to sign the agreement. The air in the hall was filled with anticipation. There wasn't room enough for everybody inside the hall, so a big crowd gathered just outside the gate.

The representative of the United Worlds was at the podium, opening the last day of the conference when a low rumbling noise was heard throughout the whole place. The audience shifted in their seats and murmured nervously.

The noise repeated, this time stronger. The floor and chair trembled under me. What is going on? I thought in panic. Earthquake? Sonic boom? Or attack? I didn't want to take chances. I jumped to my feet, forgetting to move with dignity. I ran towards an entrance to the underground nuclear shelter.

"Grell, Kim, follow me," I cried. Liss! Where was Liss? I saw her there in the front row and ran to her, grabbing her hand and dragging her to her feet.

At this moment, the cupola of the hall split in half and the whole place collapsed over our heads. There was no doubt in my mind now that it was an attack, to prevent us from signing the agreement. To prevent peace. Probably someone from the arms business. threatened with losing his high income. I thought, as I ran to the shelter, Liss running behind me. We were helping other people find their way to the shelter in the chaos and confusion caused by the explosion.

Thick smoke filled the place. My eyes watered.

Liss stumbled and coughed. The entrance was only a few yards away. Stones, broken glass and debris was showering upon our heads. Cries of pain could be heard from the crowd. Some delegates were knocked off their feet. But an amazing thing happened. The frightened crowd didn't stampede blindly. Somebody would always lean over a fallen creature and help.

I saw citizens of Amerronda carrying the unconscious citizens of Sovidjan to safety. I saw citizens of Sovidjan wipe blood from the faces of the Amernais and protect them with their own bodies, dragging them away from the raging flames. Everyone tried to help each other, forgetting the differences and past quarrels. In the face of the emergency, we were all the same, all with equal rights to survive.

Liss stumbled again. I caught her in my arms like a child and carried her to safety.

But then I noticed that the old Amerindian, Grell Sardon, was wounded. Blood was gushing from his wide chest. Somebody was leaning over him. From behind I could only see the striped yellow fur and quivering ears of a Cill'Baj. The latter raised his head, looking around, and cried for help.

But everybody was busy with their own personal survival problems.

Seeing that he was on his own, Kim Gudenow -- for that was the identity of the Cill'Baj put his paws around the wounded Amernais and dragged him to the safety of the entrance to the shelter. He surprised me with the gentleness with which he handled his wounded colleague and former enemy.

We reached the entrance almost at once. I let Liss in and helped Kim to carry Grell.

A strong tremor ran through the whole collapsing building. I only hoped that the shelter would hold. I wasn't sure what kind of an explosion caused the disaster. Was there any deadly radiation? I didn't know. The stronger and uninjured ones worked together to help the less fortunate victims.

Kim Gudenow returned several times to the ruined hall, helping to rescue as many as he could. I realized that under the grave expression and conduct of the Sovidjanians, beat very sensitive and compassionate hearts, willing to help and even sacrifice themselves for a good cause.

The smoke in the halls slowly settled, leaving a terrifying picture of destruction. We knew that the rescue team must be on its way. A doctor present among the delegation of Amerronda examined Grell Sardon and announced that his wound wasn't deadly. He would live. I was greatly relieved to hear that, and I knew also that the help offered him by Kim Gudenow would seal the peace agreement much better than any signature ever would.

Tired, I sat next to Liss, put my arms around her and kissed her temples. She smiled and I forgot everything again, submerged in our love.

We returned to Rajpeeti as soon as the agreement had been signed. Grell Sardon was recovering in the clinic and the papers had been brought to him there. Doctors said that it wouldn't be too long before he could return to his presidential functions. His health was improving quickly.

He invited the delegation of Sovidjan to Amerronda, and Kim Gudenow invited him to visit Sovidjan.

The peaceful relationship between the two systems was slowly evolving. After a long investigation, the party responsible for the devastating explosion during the Peace Conference has been discovered. Just as I suspected, it was the president and trustees of the largest weapon manufacturer of Amerronda. Signing the Peace Agreement would put an end to their profits and their very existence. The guilty had been put to trial and would serve heavy sentences. Well, for some it wasn't easy to let go of the old ways. For some there was much to lose and a lot of greed and selfishness to overcome. But the changes had started and now it was only a matter of time to reach the victory. The New Golden Age was coming for the systems of Amerronda and Sovidjan. For me, it was a great satisfaction. The Governor was proud of me. Soon the post,of Vice Governor was vacated, and I was offered the honor of taking his place. I accepted, of course.

Liss gave birth to a beautiful baby boy that we named him Sid.

Years passed. I took part in many more peace assignments like the one I just described. Between Isrun and Palatia, between Salvaton and Nicazumbe, and many, many others. My message was always the same, however. For how else can we bring peace but through extending love? This is the only way.

Fifteen standard years later, I was appointed the

Governor of the galaxy. It was the highest honor and reward for my efforts that I could ever dream of. But it was also very hard work and heavy responsibility. Well, I simply had to stand up to the expectations with great help and understanding from Liss and my children, who gave me all the support they could, I carried on with my work and responsibilities for many, many years.

And now, I am a very, very old man, ready to retire, with the feeling that I fulfilled my duty to human and non-humankind. I am ready to take a break and let the others carry the burden. My memories faded like a fog and I must have fallen asleep, exhausted. What else was there to say? I just about said it all, didn't I?

EPILOGUE

There was a strange buzzing that slowly came to my attention and started to bother me a little. Something was keeping my head in an unpleasant embrace, squeezing.

What was it? Oh. yes! I remembered after a while. A Memor-Tap. I must have fallen asleep after I finished recording my life story. I felt an unpleasant throbbing in my temples, and had a splitting headache. I lifted my numb hands and removed the Memor-Tap headpiece from my head. What a relief!

I opened my eyes and looked through the window. The blue sun Koont just sat over the horizon, leaving a brilliant halo, just over the cupola of the ancient Temple of Light.

The red sun was still high on the sky, but I liked the subdued light of this late hour very much, with gold and purple coloring the city roofs, casting a pleasant magenta hue over everything it illuminated.

For a long while, I just lay there in my suspension force field enjoying the magnificent sunset. A feeling of deep satisfaction spread through my entire being. I felt happy. My mission accomplished, my memories recorded, I was at last a free man, able to do as I pleased.

I looked up at the sky again. The traffic was still heavy above the City. Oh, well, what else is new? I will just have to beat it. From here to my country estate was only half an hour by Tolux. I knew that Liss was waiting for me there with a small family celebration.

After all, it was an important day of my life. Today, I ended my career as a Governor and began the normal life of an ordinary citizen. I would have so much time now to do all the things I always wanted to do; at last I could dedicate myself to what I wanted to do for so long and never had time enough. I wanted to compose music, write poetry, do the advanced prana-otani meditation leading to illumination of the soul, and travel in the astral to other nonphysical dimensions. Oh! There were so many things to do. Who said that retirement must be dull? Who said that it has to be an end of active life? It seems that for me it's going to be only a beginning.

My headache disappeared. The feeling of excitement and well-being took over.

I disentangled myself from the suspension field and punched the button at my personal control unit to call the Tolux. There were some papers on my desk, but I decided to ignore them. I was in a holiday mood. Let Grakkan, my successor, worry about it. I was really proud of him. He was a SNYX, too, of course, and a very talented one. I was sure that he would carry my office with dignity and do an excellent job. It was his turn now.

My control unit buzzed, letting me know that my Tolux was waiting for me outside. Good. I cast a last look at my office without regret. It was time to go.

I went slowly to my Tolux, punched the coordinates on the computer, and let the automatic pilot deal with the traffic jam. I closed my eyes and must have dozed again.

After all, it had been a long day. I had a strange dream. I saw the whole galaxy, its millions of star systems, suns and planets, all interconnected, bridged by beams of brilliant luminous opalescent light, uniting and binding the galaxy together.

I looked at it in astonishment. What is this light? I wondered. It was extraordinary! Fantastic !!!

I watched the majestic spectacle in awe. Then I realized what it meant. It was me who had built this network of light, the bridges between the worlds. I had built it with my love. Every place in the universe that I sent my unconditional love during my long work in the service of humanity and nonhuman intelligences was marked by the patch of brilliant light. Did I really do it? Did I really create this beautiful model of the binding force of the Universe?

Deep inside me I knew that it was true. It was my creation. I woke up with a start the moment my Tolux touched the landing strip behind my estate. I had a feeling that I had forgotten something. Something important. I shook my head slightly, trying to remember what it was. And then in one flash of recognition, I knew what it was. I wanted to leave a message to a specific young man in the galaxy. I put my Memor-Tap back on my head quickly. Here it goes: If you, young man, are different from the others around you, if they call you a freak, a misfit, a weirdo, and other names only because you are not like the rest -- don't worry about it. You see -- there might be a possibility that you are one of us -- a SNYX .... "